THE
AVIAN
GOSPELS

BOOK I

THE
AVIAN
GOSPELS

BOOK I

ADAM NOVY

Short Flight / Long Drive Books
a division of HOBART

SHORT FLIGHT / LONG DRIVE BOOKS
a division of HOBART
PO Box 1658
Ann Arbor, MI 48106
www.hobartpulp.com/minibooks

Library of Congress Control Number: 2010928428

ISBN: 978-0-9825301-2-2

Printed in the United States of America

First Edition

Inside text set in Georgia;
title and chapter numbers in Garamond

for Adam Levin

*It's hard to convince people
you're killing them
for their own good.*
Molly Ivins

A cage went in search of a bird.
Franz Kafka

*O*ur God surpasses the Gypsy god; He is more avuncular and noble, though some of us begrudgingly admit their god is more assertive than our God, whom we haven't seen or heard from since He rose from His own corpse and promised to rescue us from peril, and He has, though in secret, and if you could witness His wondrous methods you surely would fizzle in awe, so decent and grand is He, our Savior, who speaks in a voice that is no voice, not the song of any bird, not the snap of burning logs or crunch of shoes on sand. God's voice is silence, the silence beyond silence, the noise beyond noise, the darkest of the darkness, the inner soul of light. Yet, we have come to see their god as a local force to reckon with, and so we have arrived at a practical détente. We do not pay homage to this junior divinity, this petty and vindictive astral despot, this bureaucrat, slumlord and smiter of hope, we simply acknowledge he is there, though the mere fact of his thereness confirms the scandal of being there, and vindicates our God, who, instructively, is not there, is not only not there, but is nowhere near there, is anywhere but this tainted, soiled and sold-out world of matter. We assay their demiurge with irony and ardor; his powers are apparent, we are desperate for life.

1　　*And so, the endless war finally ended. Hungary tired of slaughtering us, and we them, though, in truth, slaughter came more naturally to them, which unpleasantly surprised us, we*
5　　*thought we were great at slaughtering. When the good news arrived, we poured into the streets, dancing and singing and carrying flags. Few of our streets could be marched on, though, for most had been destroyed, and lay beneath rub-*
10　　*ble. All of us, it seemed, had seen buildings come down, cobblestones flying, livestock hurled into the sky by explosions, soaring pigs, fragments of neighbors' homes blown through our walls; most of us had seen our possessions turn to ash, had*
15　　*stood atop the heaps of shattered heirlooms. We tried to salvage books and maybe chairs, but as for pianos, grandfather clocks, tables, beds and mirrors, few of these objects survived. We soon forgot the details of these blasted belongings, the*
20　　*blemishes, inscriptions, and little private histories, we even forgot the scent of rubble, though, most nights, we stand beside these ruins in our dreams, the music of forgetting in our ears.*

　　It's true that we had suffered, yet there were
25　　*days when pain seemed distant as we waited in bread lines or for updates from the front, our children playing at our feet as we observed with that mix of pride and dread that parents have. Some of us even held cookouts or parties, while*
30　　*others formed teams or wrote poems beneath*

oaks, though this we discouraged, or tried to discourage, though the more we discouraged it, the more people did it, so then we ignored it. That worked better. There was always music playing, always a band of trumpets, trombones, tubas and drums, saxophones and fiddles, and, for the men, a belly dancer; the instruments manned by Gypsies, and how we hated Gypsies, and suspected them of things, and wished they would bathe, though few had running water, they all lived in ghettos. We so needed music in those days, and still do; the Gypsies play better than us, but that only demonstrates the emptiness of experts. Fluency in the songs of God does not bring you close to God, only in the poverty of meekness before Him can you feel His awesome force, which can't be captured in song. We are not a musical people; music is their god, their temptation, their blasphemy; music is frivolous, fatuous, sacrilegious, though if you are standing in a goulash line, or working, relaxing after work, making love or praying; if you face hardships, music can soothe you, providing you know its low place in God's scheme.

The parade at the end of the war was not grand, like those of the past, with ranks of cheering citizens and proud, resplendent soldiers. We scrambled from our lean-to's and foxholes, waving flags and humming, the melody growing in volume with our numbers, a widow here, some children there; the civic leaders gathered in what remained of the government building, just the façade of that once-proud, two-block long, canary-colored edifice, a smoke-slaked wall alone among the wastes, the columnar porticos blown out like missing teeth. When our soldiers returned, we lined the few passable streets and stood atop the handful of buildings, rejoicing. Revelers hung from light-posts or scurried up drainpipes, all of us hoisted toasts to God and hurled confetti, even the Gypsies, whose numbers increased by the day.

There was one woman who resembled a Gypsy but swore she was a Swede; this maybe-Gypsy milled about the crowd with her husband, following the melodies of our songs, but not the words, for the Swedes had just arrived and, unsure of everything, affected to enjoy local customs, though they didn't comprehend or even know them. We will assimilate, they'd said during their journey through the woods, across battlefields and mountains, prairies and rivers, stepping over bodies, the whole Earth a cemetery, all the aquifers clogged with bodies, and nearly every brook and stream and creek dammed with corpses, the stars their distant weak companions, their child so near to birth.

I think it's time, she said on the day of the parade; she'd known for hours, and had tried to hide the pain from her husband, for what with the fes-

tivities, to make a scene would be dangerous. She
couldn't bear the throes of birth, and squeezed
her husband's wrist. Pain came in thrusts as they
shoved through the crowd, it stomped the air
from her lungs. Her husband was so fragile, he
wept at any setback, a gentle man, The Gentle
Birdkeeper; Hey gentle birdkeeper, she said, I'm
about to have this baby. She leaned against him
and he helped her through the crowd to the aban-
doned storefront café they had claimed as their
home, where she lay on the table and bit her own
hand to keep from screaming.

Her husband looked scared. What should I
do, he asked. Tell me to push. Push! Push! She
pushed. He rummaged behind the counter and
found a pitcher of water, which he brought her,
What am I supposed to do with this? I don't know,
it seemed like the right thing to do, bring you wa-
ter. AAAAAHHHHHHH! she cried, Honey, tell
me what are we to do, are you okay?

I'm fine, she said, between the blasts of pain,
find a knife, you'll need it to cut the lifeline. She
could hardly get the words out, so great was the
pain, which erupted in regular bursts. Together,
they had endured storms, bandits, battlefields,
interrogations, natural formations too strange
to name, hidden jets of steam and boiling mud,
only for her to lay on this table, a parade out-
side, her husband behind the counter, searching
for a knife. They had been the objects of scrutiny

since arriving. No one who traveled the wilder-
ness was safe, anyone who survived it seemed in
league with its dangers. Her husband returned
with a knife. She squeezed his hand through the
latest crescendo, the edges of her vision redly
blurring. Perhaps you will blend in without me,
she thought, but didn't say it, he wouldn't take
it well, he didn't take anything well, though he
tried hard, his intentions were good, she did
love him, he'd done everything he could for her,
God knows it had not been much. The pain came
again, she fought it by screaming and clutching
her husband, trying to keep the darkness at bay
for long enough to have the baby.

It won't be long now, she thought. I'm scared,
he thought.

What was he going to do without her, she
wondered. The storefront café where they lived
was no place for a baby. Where would her hus-
band get food? The agony came again; the inter-
vals were shrinking, too brief now to be inter-
vals, or even pauses; moments, maybe. Breaths.
She would've said she loved him if such words
did not embarrass her, and what the hell did any
of this matter now, she was shrieking, shriek-
ing, sweating, thank God the noise of the parade
drowned the sound, Get over there and be ready,
she gasped, he left her side and bent before her
womb, her throat felt shredded, she wouldn't
need it anymore, she pushed, she pushed, oh God,

there it was, her husband had it, he lifted it, Slap
it like I told you, he slapped it. Harder, she said, it
has to cry. We only know it's living if it cries. He
slapped harder, on its hip; terrified, as ever, by
the ruthlessness of life. The baby cried. It's a boy,
he said. She felt a smile bleed across her face, so
odd a feeling. Already, color seeped from the flat
plane of her vision as if sucked by a straw.

But we do not weep at your untimely death,
Swede; you who were unchained from your body
and freed, as from an Egypt of the soul. It is we
who are doomed, and you who are released,
we who, spirit-corpses, toil beneath the living,
brandishing our phantom-knives at plethoras of
nothing, and you who see the Earth from above,
clenched and pulsing, like a sparrow's heart.

1 Seventeen years later came the strange and extravagant birds' nests, the heaps of sticks and bark and rocks like haystacks in the trees. Then the flicker of larks and sparrows,
5 the profusion of mergansers, terns, auks, shorebirds, hummingbirds, ospreys, magpies, chickadees, blackbirds, bluebirds, orioles, buntings, grosbeaks, waxwings, warblers, mockingbirds, wrens, thrushes, juncos, coots, cuckoos, kingfish-
10 ers, doves and owls, bending our branches and spattering the air with their songs as we pushed our baby strollers down the boulevards, we had so many children then, the cemeteries' tumult had gone silent. We had never given too much thought
15 to birds until that Sunday on the Steps, when a pulsing flock of hoopoes blotted out the sun, a hundred thousand cardinals in the Square like a sea of dried blood. They overflowed our city in a day.

20 Barn swallows swirled above and sang in the arena, spilling through a fissure in the ceiling; egrets pranced by the doorway like guards, their twitching eyes fixed on all who entered. Inside, many citizens debated what it was that
25 brought the birds. The Professor sparked his pipe and said, They have nowhere to live, with all the trees chopped down for fire or killed like bystand-

18

ers, our ancient forests now are fields of stumps. From the cheap seats, the Gypsies cried out that the birds were the souls of the dead. The Priest insisted that the soul is not a bird.

What is the soul, we asked.

The soul, he said, is a mist which haunts our bodies, and, unleashed by death, ascends to heaven's azure fields.

Insulted, the Gypsies departed the arena. They made to engage the birds, building yellow birdhouses and troughs of food and water, donning scraps of purple velvet no bird could resist. Often, we saw Gypsies tracking single birds, running beneath and pleading, My beloved husband/ brother/mother, I've missed you all these years, I kept the crimson quilt you made, your favorite chair, your slippers. The Gypsy ghetto teemed with relics of the past: drawerless dressers, legless chairs, non-reflecting mirrors. Above, the birds would make their noises, pretending not to notice. Maybe the dead don't see the living, or maybe they do but don't answer, or maybe the birds were not the dead at all; the Gypsies still persisted, hoisting heirlooms and children.

It's true that we were troubled by the odd birds in our yards, our squares and public places seemed like campgrounds for these creatures. How could we adjust to the waist-high walls of titmice at our doors, or finding pheasants in our cupboards? Beyond the matter of the smelly globs of their excreta, we were hopelessly unsettled by the foreign, yet seductive, Gypsy notion that the birds were our parents, or our lovers, or our children, or our enemies, or our soldiers from the war. Priests had warned in sermons that to address the birds was blasphemous. Thus did we feel torn when a bird rubbed its beak on our shoes, or mussed our hair with its wing. Some of us engaged the birds with mumbles, whispering from park benches at lunch, or out our windows, or when we raked the yard. The chirps, once a source of comfort and diversion, scared us now. Some lost their tempers and hacked down trees, or drove off birds with guns. Peals of gunfire were common again, but this time, the targets were birds. Bodies of birds packed gutters and sidewalks, children would plead with their fathers to not go out and shoot. Worse than the birds were the bullets that missed them. Many were killed by aimless rounds, mostly other hunters, old men plagued by buzzards, while the rest of us cowered in basements.

Our streets were filled with undesirable entertainers, mostly Gypsy minstrels. Of all the instrumentalists, acrobats, contortionists and jesters, tambourine players and flautists, two stood out: a father and his son who controlled the birds. We thought they were Gypsies but the father swore they weren't. Don't let our green eyes and red hair fool you, he said, we aren't Gypsies, but Swedes. The man had come seventeen years ago with his wife, who'd died giving birth on the day of the parade. His son stood at the center of the birdsea, like one about to drown, and yet the birds would do his bidding, and those who saw his drawn and jagged face amid the fire-colored cardinals and soot-black smoke of crows gazed in awe, for who can look away from one untouched by an inferno?

The Bird Boy, for that is what we called him, performed at the base of the Spanish Steps, a wide golden staircase that swept from the fountains to the shops and restaurants above, so the eaters and the shoppers saw the boy and his birds. Birds he controlled would go flat against the sky, like a sheet; they took shapes of flowers, cats, trees, of feet marching down a confetti-drenched street, of flags and joyous faces, flames, shifting clouds. The show often ended when a ghost made of birds became a massive bird of birds.

The Bird Boy drew his biggest cheers by doing portraits of the audience. His father wanted cloying likenesses of babies and their mothers, but the boy liked to tangle their faces and bodies, contort and twist their images into visages unimagined. But his father insisted he be kind, and make friends. Embarrass or insult them and they'll kill us, he said. Give them what they want, and thank them for their money. The Bird Man, as we called him, seldom actually performed. He only supervised and worried.

Among the birdshow's most devoted fans was a girl who always came with her mother. A closer look revealed them as the wife and daughter of Judge Giggs, whom the Bird Boy recognized from a portrait he had seen throughout the city. Once, we had admired Mrs. Giggs, but then her son Charlie had been killed in the war, and grief had transformed her. She hardly spoke to anybody now. Her hair had gone the white of spiderwebs, her face and her demeanor gray. She seemed possessed by all the sadness we had labored to repress; we would have shunned her if she hadn't shunned us first.

Mrs. Giggs obsessed over Katherine, her daughter, and lavished her with kisses on the forehead, and always had her arms around the girl. To protect her, we supposed, to keep her from the world and to keep the world from her, though Katherine tried to wriggle free. Mrs. Giggs also had a son named Mike, a celebrity bully who robbed the poor and gave to himself. Mike's age was in dispute, on account of certain underachievements, which made it advantageous, for publicity's sake, to say he was nineteen, when in fact he was more like twenty-three. He skulked around the city with his friends, a soldier like his father and his brother. It was fifteen-year-old Katherine on whom Mrs. Giggs would dwell, whose hand she clutched, whose hair she smoothed, whose ears she filled with warnings.

Katherine loved the Bird Boy with a love that blushed itself beyond her efforts to conceal it, a love she did not choose, an overwhelming crush, her heart shot by an arrow, bleeding and rejoicing in its ache. She could not look at him enough. She'd seen him by chance on a visit to the city, and now she had to see him every day.

Katherine's father, Charles Giggs senior, was our ruler. We called him the Judge, because he liked the name, and whatever he liked, we liked. The Judge enforced his will with methods we prefer to not disclose at this time. Just be glad you never met him. The Giggs clan was old, rich, sad. They had ruled for many generations.

The boy with the power over birds was Morgan. He was named to assimilate. His father was Zvominir, named in Sweden, long ago. The mother's name was never said, by them or us.

The streets of the ghetto were so narrow that men leaped the rooftops, so narrow that a carriage wouldn't fit between the buildings, so narrow that sunlight cut the gloom of the boy's lane for only eight minutes a day; the sun a dirty nickel, nothing more. Aimless birds stirred like tea leaves overhead. The stench of spoiling garbage overwhelmed the boy. Cooking fat lay in gutters next to vegetable skins and fruit rinds. Morgan fought the rats that scurried off with his food; the rats were courageous and would snatch things from his hands; he had to be alert with his bread.

A trio of wealthy, well-dressed boys, among them the bully, Mike Giggs, stalked the Bird Boy sometimes as he left the Spanish Steps before dinner, chasing him through smoky streets at dusk. They squeezed him by his throat until he purpled, took his money. Mostly he escaped them, but not always.

One day, a group of whooper swans alerted Morgan that the trio would attack. They swooped down from a roof and squawked like mad, and Morgan quickly looked around and saw the boys heading for him, smiling with their fists clenched. Bystanders scrambled away, for they recognized Mike from the portrait, and because he often mugged them, too. But the swans bailed Morgan out, they had warned him, and he had just a big enough head start to escape. He made the swans follow from above—they had started to fly off—until he reached safety.

That night, he told his father what had happened: the swans had saved his life. They loved him, he said, they had helped him, they had actually communicated.

The Bird Boy, the Bird Man and the swans were all in the café. Morgan had brought the birds inside. It seemed he had adopted them. Zvominir said he'd tried to talk to birds many times, and to treat them like humans, but it never worked, they were beasts who simply followed orders. He didn't want to hurt Morgan's feelings, only clarify some

factual misconceptions, but Morgan pouted. Keep
it down, he said, the swans will hear.

Sounds of crashing drew the Swedes to the
kitchen, where the swans were rooting through
the garbage, looking for food. They were giant,
and the café wasn't big enough for them, so Morgan
marched them through the streets to the
fountains by the Steps, or tried to march them,
but their feet weren't made for land, so they flew,
and he met them there. Their orange, webbed feet
were his favorite thing about them, along with
their chins, and their ticklish long necks, and of
course their total loyalty, which he swore he would
return by protecting them forever. The fountain
was their home, he announced to the fifty-odd
pedestrians who looked. They are my defenders,
and I am theirs. Bystanders knew he was the Bird
Boy, and looked at him with fear. He landed the
swans in the fountain, where they splashed like
happy children.

The fountain was a large sky-blue pool, with
nymphs of concrete and a giant ivory clamshell at
one end. When Morgan made the swans hover low
above the surface, they could tease the water into
rising. With the setting sun, the fountains looked
aflame with molten light.

He fed them every day, buying the food with
money earned in birdshows, while he and Zvominir went hungry. He also gathered other swans
around the city to join his tribe, and gave them all

names: Harry, Rupert, Hector, Heathcliff, Lavernius, Courtney, Melody, Elodie, Eloise, Dwayne.
Lavernius and Heathcliff were young, and didn't
yet know how to fly, their feathers still partly fur.
Morgan considered the swans his best friends.
They foster understanding in the city, he told his
dubious-looking father. My audience loves them.

The swans could juggle racquetballs on their
beaks; they could tangle up their necks and hover
in the sky like a many-pointed star. People loved
to see their water flames at sunset. They made
pyramids, and children posed on top.

Practicing with birds let Morgan learn the
limits of his power. He could make a bird do anything, from about a mile away, as long as he could
see them, he could make them fly in any manner
he could think of, or make them migrate from the
city for up to three days, though they always came
back, probably for the reason they had showed up
in the first place, not that he or Zvominir knew
what that was. Zvominir's power was slightly
greater, his use of it more circumspect.

Gypsies whispered to each other in amaze-
ment. They had venerated birds for all the history
of their tribe, and prayed to birds every day, but
had no prophecy or liturgy foretelling of this power. Were Zvominir and Morgan prophets? Were
they men? Were they gods?

Zvominir's fear for Morgan never ceased to
make his chest hurt; fatherhood, for him, was like

26

a wound that never healed. The boy did nothing without passion. He feared he'd made his son crave danger just by trying to protect him, when all he'd meant to do was keep him safe, as if a parent's love could but have the reverse of its desire.

The Bird Man had been born in a land called Sweden, far away from our city. His village had been razed, his people scattered through a world inhospitable; his wife had died before his eyes. Every single thing that he had loved had been destroyed except his son. His face scared almost everyone, all horizontal wrinkles, shadowed hollows, like a cliff worn down by weather, his green eyes wide and terrified and ringed by circles dark enough it seemed he was a door to the abyss.

Zvominir sat with Morgan for dinner in the storefront café where his wife had given birth. They dined at the table she had died on.

You shouldn't provoke the boys who chase you, said his father.

I don't provoke them. They beat me up and steal my money. Why are you blaming me?

They're afraid, with the trauma of the birds.

They're not afraid at all. They're kicking the shit out of me.

Every night, they said a prayer for Morgan's mother.

What was Mom like, Morgan asked.

She was fearless, Zvominir said.

Zvominir himself wasn't fearless. He worked

the buffet table at the ruins of the old government building, which Hungary had half-destroyed, and which served as a museum and event space, a testament to the Judge, and the reign of his family. Ceremonies were held there every day, where Zvominir served potatoes and made no eye contact. He smiled at his boss until his cheeks hurt. He was scared. Officials scared him, Gypsies scared him, his own son scared him; everybody scared him, including the birds.

Nothing scared Morgan.

It had taken years to clear the ruins, and people from the slums had done the work, including Zvominir and Morgan. The Swedes had moved wreckage, they'd hauled rubble on their backs, or, on lucky days, in wheelbarrows, inhaling smoke from fires that had burned for years, cinders so opaque that the sky had seemed decayed, a roof that might collapse and crush them all. There had been no horizon line to speak of in those days, only smog-banks that feasted on a wilderness of smoke trunks, smog-plumes throbbing like ventricles above, the sky and sun concealed, the soot-dark Swedes so black it seemed they'd crawled through fire. They had carried concrete chunks of every size, and also sculptures, antiquities, conference tables, paintings, thrones, hutches, fishtanks, frescoes, bureaus, bookcases, candelabra, chandeliers and proscenium arches, all of them catalogued and cleaned, tagged and wrapped in

THE AVIAN GOSPELS

velvet pillows, shrouded in red and black canvas sheets, loaded onto chariots and carried off to unknown destinations.

When Morgan was a baby, the Bird Man tied him to his back and went to work, and chased off all the birds of the city—whose numbers still were normal then—to keep the boy from knowing of the power. When Morgan grew too old to be carried, his father always kept him close, and when the boy turned seven, he worked instead of going to school. When the excavations ended, in Morgan's thirteenth year, he washed dishes in the kitchen by the ruins, until he turned seventeen, and the bird-hordes arrived. Now, for two weeks, he'd done bird tricks, and his audience increased every day.

Four days after Morgan had been saved by the swans, Zvominir worked at the site, with his ladle and soup-pot. He was yanked from his post and led by two soldiers to a tent. The Bird Man felt the usual terror, no less intense for its ubiquity. He couldn't keep track of all the cities he had fled, the beatings he'd suffered or places he'd hidden, the times he'd stuffed rags in his own mouth to keep quiet, the reeds he had breathed through to stay underwater, the trees he had climbed and lived in, the weeks he had gone without food or water, the nights since the death of his wife he'd not slept for crying. The first soldier's features were mangled and angry, as if he'd chosen to be mean because he looked mean, the other's face was scabbed, perhaps from shaving. A tiny nest of hairs grew from his chin, a weedy tangle.

The soldiers served in the army of the Judge. They were RedBlacks. They controlled the city.

Inside the tent, Zvominir sat on a stool of red and black. A broad man in robes sat across a folding desk; atop it was a vase of fake blue flowers. This man was the Judge. His features seemed bold and sharp for one so old, as if he'd willed his face into vitality, as though you could be ruthless with your face, and why not, he was ruthless with everything else. He peered sideways at Zvominir, who'd prayed to never have this meeting, and shook so much he seemed to blur.

My people have been spying on you, said the Judge. Their reports are hard to believe. A Red-Black pinned the Bird Man's hand to the table, and the Judge hit his thumb twice with a hammer.

I'm fucking suspicious of you, said the Judge, while Zvominir clenched his wrist in pain, the thumb too sensitive to touch. Did you cause this bird-invasion? The Bird Man swore he hadn't, he was just a lowly caterer whose goal in life was not to die. If I find out you're lying, said the Judge, and here he made all kinds of threats involving Morgan, and what horrors would be visited upon him while Zvominir observed. In sum, the Judge concluded, you will learn what it is like to lose a son.

Zvominir begged for Morgan's life; his thumb was bleeding, and his thumbnail was gone, it was probably on the floor. My people say that you control the birds, said the Judge. Make them leave now and I'll spare him. The Bird Man said he did indeed have some control, but that birds he had banished from his neighborhood returned after two or three days. Not the same birds, necessarily, but birds just the same. It appeared to be a cycle, like tides. He could merely shuffle them around; he was something like a maid, who cleaned a mess that always re-appeared.

The gathered RedBlacks groaned; they'd hoped the birds could be disposed of. This bird thing is a ploy, said the Judge, a get-rich-quick scheme. Isn't it? He took a pistol from his holster and held it to Zvominir's head. The Swede began to cry. You won't get a cent from me, understand?

The Judge began to clean his gun with his robe, then gave it to a RedBlack and told him to clean it. For now, he told the Bird Man, I'll pay you with your life. Don't try renegotiating, you'll get a raise when I trust you. Zvominir didn't know what he'd be paid for, exactly, but he didn't dare to ask. Instead, he composed himself and thanked the Judge.

My daughter watches your son do his routine in the *Piazza*, said the Judge. I think the act is bullshit, frankly, but Katherine loves it, and my wife and I love my daughter, and I do what I have to do to keep my wife from crying. She blames me for everything, not that I care, of course, I don't blame myself. For now, I'm blaming you. Do you have a wife?

My wife is dead.

Well then. You will come to my house and do your birdshow for my daughter, on a trial basis. Make it rated G, keep her happy, and don't piss off my wife if you can help it, I know I can't. Keep in mind how hot I am to kill you. I live about an hour from the center of town. I don't know where you slither back to at night, but I assume it's in the slums with the other Gypsies.

I am no Gypsy, and nor is my son. We're Swedes.

Swedes.

Yes, sir. Sweden is a narrow and dignified country, surrounded by mountains and water.

What the hell are Swedes doing here, he asked his men. They shrugged; they hardly knew what Sweden was, and cared even less. If your Gypsy kid steals from my house, said the Judge, I'll have him killed.

My son is no Gypsy, we're from Sweden, and I assure you that—

The Judge stood and said, If you get rid of the birds forever, I might pay you. Do good work and you could make a decent living for a mud-person. A soldier handed Zvominir directions to the house.

Meanwhile, across town, the boys were chasing Morgan again. His pursuers ran quickly, no doubt because they ate well, and their shoes were colorful and thick, while Morgan went barefoot. He had seen up close the teeth these boys possessed; rows of perfect white enamel, straight as tiles. If he hadn't memorized the streets—the pushcarts, witch doctors, minstrels, beggars, cripples, birdbaths, oil slicks and cultists—the bullies would have robbed him again. He dove beneath a moving carriage and clung to its axel, throwing his arms and legs around it and riding out of danger, riding for countless city blocks, through garbage, shit and puddles, until he was sure there was no way they had followed him. When the carriage slowed, he tumbled to the ground. He was in a neighborhood he didn't recognize, though it looked just as awful as the others, and he refused to ask for help or get directions. He despised any kind of assistance, and would use his intuition. He had jumped into dumpsters and sewers. Anything was preferable to the twin humiliations of getting caught or looking weak. The deeper into the ghetto he lured his pursuers, the closer to quitting they got. Someday, he knew, he would reach the city's edge, and would have to turn and fight his way back. For now, he didn't know where the city stopped, and it took almost two hours to get home. His father, who had started cooking dinner in the café's back-room kitchen, a space as cramped and airless as a coffin, kissed him many times and inquired what had kept him.

They chased me.

Again?

Yes. And they're not going to stop, unless you let me kill them.

You can't kill anyone, Morgan. They'll catch you and string you up.

They'll string me up anyway. At least this way I can defend myself.

Zvominir shook his head and thought, I hope he outgrows this. Morgan thought, just wait until I'm old enough to make my own decisions. Then, anybody who looks at me wrong is dead.

Zvominir told Morgan about their new job with Judge Giggs. Morgan said he did not want to be someone's personal entertainer. Just because they're rich doesn't give them the right to have more fun than poor people, he said. Plus, it's the Judge's own son who chases me. It could lead to decent money, Zvominir said, if we prove ourselves. Money is a trap, Morgan said. The Judge will have us killed, Zvominir said. I hate life and would like nothing more than for it to end, Morgan said. Admit that it is one humiliation after another. You like your swans, Zvominir said. I am a swan trapped in a human, Morgan said. You will go with me to the Judge's house, Zvominir said. Mom is lucky she didn't live to see this, Morgan said. You are so young, Zvominir said. If youth

means I still think life should be just, then yes,
Morgan said, I am young.

They set out in the morning for the Judge's
estate, through streets crammed with soothsayers,
orphans, and homeless, crippled veterans with
their wooden limbs, milky eyes and empty beggar's cups, past the fountain, with a pause to see
the swans, up the Spanish Steps and beyond City
Hall, through the gauntlet of Gypsy entertainers.
They hitched a ride on a carriage heading out of
town, to the country, through sloping fields of tril-
lium and iris, jessamine and honeysuckle glitter-
ing in the flats, a blossom-ghetto where a grassy
hill could ramble without fetter from a building.
The *clop* of hoofbeats faded flatly in the air, and
the sky, which Morgan hadn't seriously considered until now, had shed its aspect of brown; the
blue seemed specific and crystalline, secretive,
yet immanent; intimate, yet cold. The sun, which
from his street resembled a spat-out wad of gum,
did not seem dull and faded here, but yellow and
painful to look at. As with dreams, things seemed
too big and strange to be real. Morgan fought the
peaceful sentiment spreading through him like
blood in water; he thought, just because it's pretty
here doesn't mean I want to be rich. But riotous
birdsongs pierced his resistance; he'd never seen
so many unwounded birds, birds with crests and
ruffled manes, crowns of green and purple. Because it was immaculate and safe in the country,

fancy birds abided with their features still intact, undamaged by the city.

They found themselves on a boulevard lined with homes behind tall gates, the elms and cedars sagging beneath the weight of birds, bits of chairs and tables wedged between the branches. Morgan incredulously recognized these items as parts of massive nests.

What are those birds, Morgan asked, his shock and awe religious.

The fierce-looking brown ones are hawks, said his father. And the black ones are ravens. The giant ones that look like they could carry you off are eagles.

Finally, the birds piled high enough they ceased being flocks. They were lakes, and the carriage like a boat, the only people who could part the sea its passengers. No human being could live in these conditions very long without going mad. Perhaps, thought the Bird Man, the birds were worse here than in the city because the air and land were clean, while the city was a filthy toxic blot upon the globe, a megadump.

The Swedes jumped off the carriage and thanked the driver. An ostrich approached them on spindly legs, its bearing made it seem like an ambassador. Morgan tickled it chin. Zvominir followed the instructions on the sheet the soldier had given him, while Morgan controlled the eagles with arcing gestures. He felt a bit afraid of these monsters, yet they obeyed all his commands, he could make them do anything. For now, they did cartwheels on the edges of their wings.

A group of RedBlacks stood guard by the high stone gate of the Giggs house, surrounded by thousands of giant and laconic birds of prey, confident and taut in their power, like the Judge himself. They may have chosen his house because of him, though perhaps we only think that to inject coherent themes into the nothing of the everything. We've been expecting you, said the RedBlacks, hurry up and get rid of these fuckers. This was the worst birdflood Zvominir and Morgan had seen. Birds parted slowly enough for the Swedes to scratch some of their heads, and check their beaks and feet. They seemed fine. The building before them, which the Swedes assumed to be the Giggs house, resisted comprehension, both because the birds had engulfed it, and also for the oddness of its shape and vast dimensions. It seemed to have the weightlessness of clouds, and disappeared into the sky, and where the borders were between the two the Bird Boy and his father couldn't say.

Zvominir knocked on the towering door, above which was a red and black crest. Eagles were so plentiful here that Morgan reasoned he could make them kill the Judge.

And when the door opened, it was Katherine Giggs, the girl from the square who liked his act, who he knew from all the portraits. She concealed her blushing face, and her mother stood beside her, smiling, both happy and sad. Beside them was an angry Mike Giggs. He had the same freckles as the girl, and his hands were clenched in fists, as were Morgan's. A feeling of incredible opportunity dawned on Morgan. This job was not a chore, it was a privilege. He was entering his tormenter's home, in the capacity of savior.

Zvominir doffed his cap and went to bow, but Morgan cut him off and looked at Mike.

I'm here to entertain your sister, he said, fishing some chickadees from his pocket and juggling them. I believe it was your daddy who hired me. So get out of my way. I'm walking into your house.

2 After Morgan had shoved past Mike and smilingly stood beside Katherine, Mike punched him in the face. Mrs. Giggs cried, Don't hurt my son!, but Mike advanced and kept on punching. Zvominir rushed to save Morgan from the bigger, stronger boy. Mike's and Morgan's punches conked off Zvominir's ears while Katherine tried to wrestle off her brother.

I can take him, Morgan said. Get off me. Zvominir covered Morgan's mouth with his hand.

Stop it, Katherine said. I hate you.

You're taking his side, Mike asked. I'm telling Dad.

Dad hired them, dummy.

You're lucky my sister saved you, Mike said, pointing at Morgan. Someday, you'll be alone, and then I'll get you. He turned and ran up the steep white stairway, his arms raised in victory, crying out, Yes! Yes! He wins again! He always wins!

Morgan had been chased and punched by Mike Giggs many times, but never in front of a girl. He tried not to cry and shielded his face, shoving his father away.

Ever since his brother died, said Mrs. Giggs, he hasn't been the same. None of us have.

My mother died, said Morgan. Why is his

brother so important?

It must've been so hard on him, said Zvominir, glaring at Morgan as if to say *Shut up*.

It's been harder on me, said Morgan, bawling. He could not control his sobs.

He's so emotional, Katherine thought. No one in her family ever cried. They weren't allowed to. Her father called it blackmail. But Morgan was in torment, and his soul could only issue forth in surges. He was honest and pure. She had never stood so close to him before. She felt drunk, but knew that she must try to act the role of hostess. After all, she had begged her father to invite the magic Swedes to the house. I'm so embarrassed, Katherine said. Will you still help us?

Of course, said Zvominir. Won't we, Morgan?

Katherine gestured through the foyer to a row of distant, giant, barrel-vaulted windows shut by curtains; beyond them, Morgan felt a writhing.

We keep the curtains closed, said Mrs. Giggs.

Zvominir and Morgan strode between the walls of white that loomed and hovered, hid and reappeared, the roof too high to see and covered up by palm fronds, the trunks like massive wooden weeds. Morgan's emotions soared upward in this space, smitten by this quietude and stillness of cathedrals where nothing stirred but candle flames and all sounds seemed like accidents, only

to plunge and plunge, his emotions, for he could
feel the splendor of this room, but never own it;
how gullible and cheap he felt, and vulnerable to
ostentation.

The strange and shifting surfaces pleased
Katherine, who liked the way that voices slapped
off walls and wound their way through halls and
byways like rumors, waves of noise rippling and
splashing; she could trace their path to who had
skipped the words like stones. Mike didn't really
understand the house, or even what there was to
understand, he just liked that it was big, and that
he'd own it someday.

Zvominir, Morgan, Katherine and Mrs. Giggs
moved through watery light like fish, weaved between daybeds, stone busts and statues. The walls
were covered with shot-up mosaics that told of
the city's history: ladies and champions, monsters and villains, the victory of its heroes over
heathens, though the victories were embellished.
Lush red narrative carpets lied, too; it pains us to
admit we can't win wars, as we so love them, and
so we persist in not admitting it. They walked past
a meeting table ringed with red chairs, each with
a nameplate on its backrest.

Zvominir recognized them as relics from City
Hall. He saw the shrine to Charlie, the eldest Giggs
child, whose supposed military courage had been
famous, and still was. In this tabletop display of
little portraits, he looked young in his military

uniform, and almost out of place, as if the epaulets and boots didn't fit him. Picture after picture showed the same awkward boy, who seemed too young and sweet to be a soldier.

Mrs. Giggs parted the curtains, revealing the yard's roiling, blue-glinting dark, a sea-sized field submerged by birds, their flappings crashing like breakers, their stirrings immense, impulsive, seismic, a seascape inspired by forces unknown, and though we'd like to know the reasons for these forces, God being God, we won't. No words we could fling at His feet could cancel His right to make bird-lakes of our yards, and though we may pray, weep, beg, gnash our teeth, rip our clothes, tear our hair, shriek and cower, He and His Justice will endure, and we shall celebrate them. Morgan stood before the patio door.

We'll never go out there again, said Mrs. Giggs, shielding her daughter and dabbing at her own nose with a tissue—she always seemed to have a cold—wondering if she should've brought young lives into this world, only for their hopes to be destroyed. What could the future hold for Katherine and Mike, and how could these birds be made to leave?

Katherine was afraid, and afraid to look afraid. She would not be like her mother: scared of everything, and felt ashamed to be this close to her now, in front of other people. When the patio door was opened, the birds swam to the Swedes' feet, wriggling and abashed, forgetting how to fly, Katherine and her mother edging backwards.

They won't hurt you, Morgan said. Mrs. Giggs didn't look convinced.

Sweethearts, said Morgan, who swelled with love for every single bird. Zvominir flung up his arms, and the birds took to the sky, the vacuum they created sucked the humans off their feet, the dome of elevating birds like a rooftop blown away. A single grackle flitted into Morgan's palm, he pressed his face into its feathers and stroked its tiny wing, traded kisses with it, rubbed its beak. His father strew the million birds across the robin's egg sky, broke the bird-dome into bits, scattering their masses into thousands of directions, drenching the yard with the sunlight they'd blocked, while those below concealed their eyes. It was possible to see now how the birds had harmed the land, how the flowerbeds and fields of grass were marbled; a wide and white-gray swale of birdshit was uncovered, stinging to the noses and the eyes of the humans who seemed dotlike to this plethora of creatures.

The back yard is destroyed, said Mrs. Giggs.

My son and I could fix it, said Zvominir. It won't take so long.

It would take forever, Morgan said.

Two weeks at most. We could start today.

Zvominir conferred with Mrs. Giggs while Morgan raged; his father spoke of dates, times and shovels. He wants to make me shovel shit, Morgan thought. Stepping through the door into the sunlight, Morgan called the birds back, for they alone loved him without complication, they alone tended to his moods and indulged his desires. Hawks, eagles, ravens, vultures, jays and parrots made the yard dark again. He taxonomized them according to color and inspected them to make sure their bodies were undamaged, their beaks uncracked and wingbones strong, their feet still orange, their feathers free of harm from the likes of Mike. Katherine and her mother backed into the house, and Zvominir drove the birds away.

Morgan summoned them back.

Not now, said his father.

You're making them afraid, Morgan said. He turned to Katherine and called down a raven. Didn't you lose a brother, he asked.

Yes.

Please, don't, said Mrs. Giggs, unsure what exactly she had begged him not to do, but fearful anyway. She wished the boy and his father would go home and take their birds with them, and leave her Katherine alone.

Katherine didn't want to be as frightened as her mother. She wanted to travel and explore; the novel and exotic had made her their plaything; pictures, books and stories thrilled her. She had consumed all the books in her home; They're supposed to be accessories, said her father, Why'd she read them? Because of this, she knew things that most of us didn't: that maps in her schoolbooks were wrong, that her city was flat, provincial and small, that narrowness and ignorance were rewarded by her teachers, most of whom were less informed than her, and more capricious.

Katherine pretended that she lived in a city with clear views of the ocean, imaginary friends, weather that made her nostalgic for the future, murmurous fountains and trees that teemed with fruit, fogbound alleys of shadow and scent, buildings that inspired her to awe. Trips with her mother to the actual city included shopping, and the chance to eat desserts. Katherine liked to shop and binge on sweets, and yet. Her city, she admitted to herself, seemed picturesquely cloying, monotonously cute. Of course, she only visited the safe parts built for friends of the Judge and their children. The streets are safe to walk on! they'd preposterously announce, surrounded by a hundred RedBlack escorts, when every real city dweller knew they weren't.

She intended to travel. For reasons too complex to explain to a child, and we hope you'll shield the ears of your own children, all of our surrounding nations—China, Bolivia, Angola, Oklahoma, Kwakutil, Onandago, Susquehanna, and of course, the dreaded Hungary—all of our neighbors considered us their enemy, no doubt because we'd failed to convert them. Someday, we will look on from cloud-banks in Heaven while demons spear our neighbors in Hell, meanwhile we find ourselves surrounded, then as now, a dismal, sorry geopolitique, and not for children.

One more word on Katherine Giggs. Classmates saw her as an over-privileged non-conformist in a world where everybody else had to conform. They wore clothes that were outrageously expensive, she wore jeans and shirts from thrift-stores. They invited her to parties out of fear, and she mostly didn't go, which terrified their parents, who feared being purged. No one knew how the Judge and his wife had produced such a misfit creature, a toucan for oddness, a peacock for flourish, an owl for her big eyes and affinity for darkness.

This raven is your brother, aren't you, said Morgan as it swooped onto his arm and poked his earlobe with its beak. The bird squawked its battle-cry, a shrillness that rattled chandeliers, made windows shudder in their panes, and drove Katherine to hide behind her mother yet again, though she emerged, attempting to look bold. Having courage wasn't easy. Don't be scared, said Morgan. The bird just wants to know you. Nothing scares me, Katherine said, wishing it was true, wanting everybody to believe it. I hate that part of you, said her mother.

Katherine took a breath for strength and went to Morgan. The bird unveiled its wingspan and squawked, twisting as if wrenching from its feathers.

Don't be nervous, Morgan said. Zvominir threw his arms up and walked away, but Morgan didn't care if he was angry. Just once, he should feel the pain of compromise.

The raven was placed on Katherine's skinny arm. Its eyes rimmed with almond stopped twitching.

Ouch, Katherine said. It has claws.

You will too, one day, Morgan said.

Mrs. Giggs shook, as if the bird was actually her son.

Zvominir would end things any minute now, thought Morgan, yet he pressed on, thrilled by defiance. He led Katherine and the raven outside. The bird leaped off her arm and whizzed into the sky, soared and spun and looped back down to Katherine, who still looked dismayed as it settled on her, its talons circling her bicep like shackles.

He will always come to you, said Morgan of the raven, though he knew it wasn't true, but boasting made him happy. He took the creature off her arm, into his hands. I'll introduce you to my swans, he said. I'll teach you their names. They talked about his swans, and Katherine said she loved them, she would make them dinner, maybe get a bird-doctor for them. She would be their patron, it would bring her close to Morgan and impress him.

1   Morgan let the raven hover over Katherine. A
blast rang out above; the bird exploded. Zvominir
ran from the inside of the house to the yard, and
flung himself onto Morgan; Katherine fled inside.
5   The Swedes looked up and found a smiling Mike
Giggs in the third-story window, a smoking rifle in
his hands. The bird lay splattered on the patio, its
twitching wings still trying to fly, its life expired, a
nimbus of its feathers snowing down.

10   An eagle screamed down, seized the rifle
from Mike's hands and nearly yanked him from
the window. Morgan squirmed out from beneath
his father and took the gun from the eagle, and
would've killed Mike if Zvominir hadn't lunged at
15   the barrel, pointing the muzzle at the house. Morgan shot. The bullet struck the house and raised
a puff of dust; Zvominir and Morgan's ears went
almost silent. Zvominir ejected the magazine and
threw the rifle into the yard, where it landed in
20   birdshit. Morgan shaped the birds into a giant
rifle, and pointed it at Mike in his window, seven
thousand two hundred twenty-six birds of prey,
each one raging wildly, awfully shrieking, jaws
open, talons stretched, temper horrid, hunger
25   violent, starved for murder.

Mrs. Giggs ordered her daughter to her room,
but Katherine stopped at the edge of the hall, listening as sound rivered around the corners.

Get out, said Mrs. Giggs.

30   He killed your son, Morgan said.

48

For god's sake, said Zvominir, Shut your mouth.

He killed your brother, Morgan said, searching with his eyes into the house for Katherine's face. Remember that it was him. You murdered your brother, he said, turning toward Mike's bedroom. Murderer!

Mike, from above, grinned and waved.

My son is not a bird, said Mrs. Giggs, and you have no idea who killed him.

3 Zvominir discovered he had the power over birds when he was eight. It arrived out of nowhere, and with no explanation; he was walking home from school and thinking of volcanoes, when every bird within a mile up and formed a volcano, and fired bird-lava, bird-ash and bird-cinders into the air. The village had a normal amount of birds, but you don't know how many birds you have until they all band together and start listening to a child. Townsfolk weren't enthused by Zvominir's display, and discouraged him from wielding the gift, which they referred to as a curse. Their methods of persuasion included flames, threats, expletives and pitchforks. You might want to listen to them, honey, said his parents, who seemed divided on whether to defend their Zvominir from the crowd, or protect themselves. In sum, birds were spoiled for the boy. We don't really blame the village: we would have done the same thing they did, but our relationship with birds was trickier.

Zvominir lived beside a forest. He hated the temptation of the birds, but loved their siren songs, and walked all day until he felt that he'd been punished, that he'd sufficiently opposed his own desire. Once, the woods had been a place of joy, but now he searched out rings of trees where birdcalls echoed, and immersed himself in gorgeous painful song, in pure refusal.

In an instance of the kind of global turbulence we don't like to dwell on, a tribe called Arizona, who lived across the border, stormed his town when he was seventeen. As the villagers lay expiring in the Square, they rued that Zvominir might have used the gift to save their lives. His parents couldn't marvel at the irony of this, in their state; indeed, they could do nothing. They were dead. I thought you said I shouldn't use the curse, said the boy, who was tied to a tree. Townsfolk tried to order him to use his common sense, if indeed he had it, and told him to intuit there were times when laws should be suspended, including and especially when lives, such as their lives, were in danger, but, no, it was too late in the day, and with their dying words they likened him to certain private regions.

Seventeen years after Zvominir came to our city, the zillion birds appeared. He thought it was a dream, or possibly a joke, but perhaps also an opportunity, and certainly a danger.

Morgan hadn't known he had the power, and neither did his father, who'd chased off every bird in his purview, to keep the boy in innocence, and to keep himself from thinking of his childhood. Zvominir called the bird-free zone around himself The Force-Field. In time, the Bird Man grew certain that his son had not inherited the curse.

Then the birds arrived and triggered Morgan, for whatever unknown reason, like a hex the gods had suddenly remembered to enforce. Several hundred thousand birds landed while Zvominir was cleaning up from breakfast. Without knowing why, he felt as though a secret crime he had committed years ago was about to be revealed, and he leaned against the wall, for he was dizzy. Morgan came inside from the street, with sparrows orbiting his head, as though he was a proton. I know this sounds crazy, he said, but I think I control them.

Zvominir shook his head and muttered, No. He tried not to cry. What's wrong, Morgan said. This is incredible.

The Swede sat Morgan in the kitchen and explained the power was a gift or a curse, depending. You knew I had this, Morgan said, and never told me? I knew I had it, said his father, I didn't know about you. To be honest, I hoped you had been spared.

Morgan ran outside to the street. Crows had huddled everywhere, like people wearing hoods, and Gypsy boys wove between them, playing *ska* on rusty instruments and kicking soccer balls. Morgan heretofore had been the object of their ridicule. On the rooftops sat a hundred thousand angry-looking falcons, and Morgan stomped into the middle of the concrete crow-strewn soccer pitch, raised his arms, and brought down rivers of the roofbirds in a fury, knocking everybody flat, himself included, the falcon-torrent blasting through the canyon of the ghetto like a dam-burst of birds. He lay upon his back and made the birds as furious as he was, and saw how effortless and total was his power. He sent the falcons back up to the rooftops, and preened in his authority. Never fuck with me again, he announced.

Zvominir dragged him off the street and apologized, but saw how many birds there were, and felt the ones he couldn't see. This was a new kind of natural disaster, something unexplainable and huge. The universe was laughing at him.

On his travels with his wife—a girl from Northbrook he'd escaped with, who'd misconstrued his traumatized anxiety for tenderness, a gaffe born of hope, which he dreaded, for how it made him love her—the allure of easy freakshow money flexed its lurid lure, but he feared to draw attention to himself, or, worse, to entertain. He hated entertainment for its flattering deceit, its unrewarding promise that a life could be fulfilling. Entertainment overstated fun, and fun was disappointment's early phase.

At dawn the next day, someone threw a Molotov cocktail at the storefront café, but they must have done it from a distance, or in haste, for it fell among the falcon mound that lay against the entrance, and made a bird inferno. Falcons tried to take the air as fire devoured them, so flames climbed the sky. Zvominir and Morgan heard the cries, and ran out to the birdfire.

Burning falcons rained in smeary yelloworange against the dark, or howled in pain on the concrete, and streaked the eyes of all who saw them. Zvominir kept his son within the doorway, to protect him, but Morgan screamed against the city walls, Who did it? Cowards! Take me on, face to face!

They're scared, said his father, in a low voice, his calmness startling to them both. Nothing comes of this gift but trouble.

The Gypsy boys who'd thrown the Molotov cocktail would be killed by their own people for murdering the birds, but that would bring no consolation to the Bird Boy. Falcons shielded him from fire with their own bodies; he felt responsible for their lives. They had been his bodyguards: they'd died for him.

Morgan took the ashes of the falcons in his hands. They crumbled into nothing as he held them.

4 They were back on the dirt road again, a father and son cast out from the Giggs house to creep back to their slum, Zvominir envisioning what they'd eat that night—nothing—Morgan lamenting the fact that his father'd betrayed him again, that he wanted to fight Mike once and for all, gunpowder still in their throats and eyes, clouds above drooping, too heavy to float, wildflowers rattling and muttering their nothings in the meadow, weeds pressed through dirt like the words of the buried, everywhere their undeciphered pages.

Zvominir told Morgan he had put his swans in danger with his temper, that the Judge would very likely have them killed now. Working for the Giggs' would've earned us privileges, he said, you could've had money for your swans. Instead, you offended the single best client you could ever hope to have. I don't want clients, Morgan said, I want a revolution, I want justice.

Justice doesn't exist, said his father.

What if his father was right, Morgan thought, and the swans were in danger? Could it be that they would die because of him? The idea was too painful and complex for his mind to contain. It made him want to fight.

A family of doves watched as they passed,

and Morgan made them fly in loops, though he felt sad. He wanted to wing far away from his body as birds flew away from the earth, yet felt trapped by the sky's azure irony: how it bluely offered vastness, yielded only lack, trapping him inside its sapphire prison; blue day, how you lie, he thought, your blue's more bleak than black. He said as much to Zvominir, who warned that he would be the remnant of his own life, as ashes were of flame.

A caravan of RedBlacks passed them on horse-back. They considered the Swedes, and twisted their moustaches. What is your kind doing here, they asked, dismounting and sticking out their muscled, armored chests, brandishing their long, shiny guns. Zvominir explained that he and Morgan worked for Judge Giggs. We, too, work for Judge Giggs, said the RedBlacks, but what could your kind do for His Honor? We help out around the house. So you're servants. You could say that. How do you serve? Zvominir gulped and said, We control his birds. The soldiers exchanged puzzled looks. Do you shoot them? No. Poison them? No. What, then? We act as emissaries. Emissaries, they said. Are you some kind of pervert? Why, no, and what a funny question. Haha, said soldiers; Zvominir also said, Haha. You must be some kind of Gypsy witch-doctor, they said. Is that skinny thing there your assistant? He's my son. Please don't hurt him.

Go ahead and try to hurt me, Morgan said. You don't scare me.

The soldiers now passed out of confusion, into wonder.

You think you're so tough, Morgan said. All of you are cowards. Fuck you. I almost killed Mike Giggs. You girls can't take me.

Shrugging, the soldiers struck the Swedes with their gun-butts, wrestled them onto their stomachs and kicked them, emptied their pockets of lint, debris, rags, calling them Gypsies, pickpockets, thieves, accusing them of stealing, subversion, black magic, spells to dupe the charitable, well-meaning populace, stomping on their knees and their ankles and their softer parts as Zvominir begged for Morgan's life, even as the soldiers picked the boy up by his feet, dangling him upside down to shake loose any contraband he might've swiped as he trawled through the suburbs with their charitable millionaires so naïve to a Gypsy beggar's wiles; tore off the rags of Morgan's shoes and searched them, ransacked his body and squeezed his prostate, and his father's; he was punched some more and kicked again, yet Morgan thrashed and spewed and kept on flailing, kicking, brandishing his teeth, and, truth be told, the soldiers liked the Bird Boy's spirit even as they tried to evict it via stomping and stuffing his mouth full of dirt, and spitting in his eyes, Zvominir's heartbeat just a shimmer and Morgan

1   staring straight at his father, crying, *I may die,*
     they may kill me on this road, but I will fight.

5 When he heard from his wife what had happened at his house with the Swedes—ac-
counts of which were various, depending
on who gave them; Mike said that Morgan attacked him, Katherine blamed Mike, and Mrs.
Giggs accused the Swedes of witchcraft, and
seemed inordinately spooked by the Bird Man
and his son, and insisted that they get the kind
of justice received by any enemy of the state; she
also seemed to blame them for knowing things the
Judge preferred to not consider, such as Charlie's
death, the mere implication of which was enough
to doom the Bird Man and his son—the Judge
sent a detachment of his RedBlacks to wait for
Zvominir and Morgan at the Steps, where they
did their act. Mike would accompany the soldiers
and watch as the duo were quickly apprehended
with a minimum of scandal and spirited off to be
killed. These were the methods of the Judge: effi-
cient and silent. Victims of this treatment were invariably Gypsies, whom none of his constituents
could stand, so he only gained support when they
were victimized. The Judge inspired fear, curried
favor, and solidified his power with the selfsame
beatings. Thrift!

It was early in the morning, and the Square
was mostly empty but for Gypsies readying their

various performances, shopkeepers sweeping off their stoops; the lavender light of a morning of smoke shadowed all in its view, with all the shadows double-shadowed, the darkness dappled by the birdclouds. Mike felt groggy from having to be up at this hour. He wore his new general's uniform, which he'd stolen from a military barracks, along with a collection of medals he'd swiped from a display case in his house. He found he tapped his foot to the sound of a Gypsy band, who played their bouncy, surging, oddly optimistic *ska*, with horns and skipping rhythms. He had heard *ska* many times, but now, it affected him differently.

A Gypsy man stood beside the band and gave them orders, like a manager or promoter, his brown suit splotched with grease, his buttonless shirt black with filth, a green shirt beneath it, pinned too tight across his chest. Yet, his green eyes were alert beneath the flourishing red weedbed of his brow. You must be important, said the man, you have shiny medals. I am, Mike said, I'm a general, and the future of this city, I'm the prince, you may have heard of me. A general and a Prince, the man said. Wow! So many titles at once, it's a wonder you can bear them all, and with such youthful shoulders! I'm not sure what that's supposed to mean, said Mike, are you insulting me? Of course not, said the promoter, and let us prove our allegiance, we shall play a song in your honor.

RedBlacks scanned the Square for the Swedes from their perch atop the Steps. The giant white swans looked at home in the fountains, smashing their way through the water in a manner that would've seemed messy if the water wasn't water, but was something more destructible, and the impunity of these creatures bothered Mike, though the music kept him calm and distracted. He found he loved *ska*.

A crowd of Gypsies and some shoppers came to listen to the music. Mike felt what he thought were the pickpocket hands of the young Gypsy boy who stood behind him. He padded the back of his pants for his wallet, and found it wasn't there, so he grabbed the boy's throat and started squeezing, screaming at this scrawny little Gypsy while RedBlacks hurried down the Steps to safeguard the Judge's only living son.

The boy could have been any age from nine to fourteen, so skinny and malnourished did he look, his hair a kind of lice-infested undergrowth. He had the same freckles had by all of them; all of them were messy-faced and twitchy. A group of Gypsy beggars prayed for mercy for the boy. Mike told the RedBlacks that his wallet had been stolen. The Gypsy boy pleaded innocence, or tried to, but his gasping wasn't recognized as speech, where a chokehold saw to that. Mike demanded vengeance, and RedBlacks needed no more provocation. They stripped the child of his dignity, right there in the Square; broke the legs off chairs and shoved them up his orifices, then complained they couldn't use him as a chair.

Take us to your father, said the RedBlacks to the boy, who thought he was Morgan. Mike did not say otherwise. He had attention span issues. The boy tried not to scream, to keep the soldiers from attaining satisfaction, so they set upon the birds in the fountain, the swans beloved by Morgan, who screamed as they were tortured. Where's your bird god now, bitch, asked the RedBlacks. Where's your bird god now?

When the Gypsy boy continued to refuse, the RedBlacks turned on Gypsies praying in the Square, and demanded the Bird Man's location. Force was deployed; rifles were used as battering devices, as probes for certain cavities, as handles for the bayonet, and, finally, for shooting. At some point, Mike found his wallet in the pocket of his stolen General's coat.

6 The Swedes had collected themselves when the beating ended, and resumed their dismal march for the city, but slowly, slowly, encumbered as they were by wounds, for which the Bird Man blamed his son, though Morgan blamed his father, whose sycophantic desperation needed to be stopped. His father hastened to remind him how his second tantrum in a day might have further doomed the swans. He only half-believed it, Zvominir, but knew his son had no response.

The walk back to the city took all night, but Morgan wouldn't rest, he feared the safety of the swans—his father's tactic worked too well—and, when Zvominir couldn't keep the pace, or didn't seem to want to, Morgan went from blaming him for being obsequious to blaming him, somehow, for the peril of his bird-friends. They entered the city at daybreak, hungry and desperate.

Hurry up, he told his father.

They headed for the fountain. Too bad Morgan won't learn a lesson, thought his father; the swans would doubtlessly be fine, no way the Red-Blacks gave a hoot about a family of birds, they must have better things to do, there were so many double-standards known as "laws" to enforce, so Morgan will continue not accepting the necessity of obedience. Too bad the swans aren't dead! Shrikes shrieked and Ural owls brooded overhead, as if pacing, clearly worried, but Zvominir assured them that everything was fine, though when he finally saw the Square, he knew why they were worried.

RedBlacks were torturing the few remaining swans in the Square, dunking their heads into fountains and holding them under, stomping on their throats, playing tug-of-war with them, or doing things with bayonets that shouldn't be described, or tinkering alone in artsy-craftsy ways. Certain soldiers posed beside their victims for portraits, blood in the fountains like wispy red smoke, the swans' disbodied feathers heaped like snow drifts. Their feet, beaks and guts lay strewn about the cobblestones. There was nothing left of them to love. Heathcliff was torn into pieces just as Morgan arrived, and Courtney, screeching, was beheaded. Eloise's eggs had been smashed, Dwayne was smoldering obscenely.

Morgan cried *No!* and called on every bird he could find to swoop down and kill the Red-Blacks. The soldiers saw this screaming boy, and wondered why he wasn't scared, but Mike cried, It's him! It's him! The RedBlacks cast a glance at the boy they'd thought was Morgan, who now lay in shreds by the Steps. Then they shrugged, and started shooting. Most of their bullets were blocked by birds, and Zvominir dove onto his son and tried protecting him, but amid the birds and shooting, Morgan took a bullet in the chest. The impact spun him sideways.

Thousands and thousands of birds zoomed in every direction, and Zvominir tried to pull his son out of the Square, though Morgan cried, Let me fight, and his father answered, I won't let you die, I won't let them kill you. Their words were lost in noise. Morgan tried to struggle free, but he was weak and bleeding, blood was everywhere, on his shirt and in his father's shoes; Zvominir's shoes were squishing. He feared his son would bleed to death. The boy kept making birds attack, but Zvominir kept stopping them, and many birds were torn in half.

He kept on telling Morgan, I won't let you die, Morgan kept on screaming. He dragged his bleeding son to a doorway, and backed through the door to a vestibule, where he laid the boy against a wall of tin-colored mailboxes. The vestibule's inner door was locked, and made of wood; he could find no way to open it. This must be some kind of apartment building, said Zvominir. Fuck that, let me fight, Morgan said. Birds absorbed the bullets fired at the doorway, an overture of massacre prefiguring the Swedes', thought Zvominir, who felt the death of every bird as a tremor in his chest. Zvominir tore his shirt off, and pressed on Morgan's wound with it. *Aiieee!* cried Morgan, What did you do that for? I'm trying to save your life.

1   Find a way to do it that doesn't hurt.

      He knelt beside his son amid a pool of blood on the gray tile floor, the door behind them locked and impossible to budge, RedBlacks drawing ever
5 closer. The Swedes had nowhere they could go, no way to escape.

7 The torrents of zooming birds that whirled in layers before the doorway where Zvominir and Morgan hid could not be shot through, thought Mike. RedBlacks stood amid the bird-storm and blasted away in all directions, and soon ran out of bullets, and sent a messenger for more, it would take about twenty minutes, which is why Mike grew impatient, we think, and fired the bazooka, though we should state for the record that we don't know for sure if it was Mike. And while it used to be against the law to blame a Giggs, now it isn't, so now we blame Mike.

No one really cares who we blame or what we say these days, or even knows we're here.

Mike had never fired a bazooka—we're not quite sure where he got it—and he found that bazookas were more tricky to control than he'd imagined. This must be why he missed the building where the Swedes had taken shelter, and hit the building next to it, which exploded and collapsed, blasting out brick-chunks in every direction and flattening RedBlacks and bystanders. Birds were killed as well, their feathers driven deep into the buildings.

Now the building where Zvominir and Morgan hid was blocked, not by birds, but by a rubble-hill, which no amount of shooting would dislodge.

The heavy wooden door which the Swedes had failed to move had toppled inward, the plaster of its doorframe having shattered with the blast. Zvominir and Morgan heard screams from the street, and fled through the newly-open doorway, to a lobby, past a fallen shattered chandelier, across a broken mirror on the floor, their shocking sooty bloody faces gaping up at them like filthy, desperate strangers. Zvominir had more of Morgan's blood on him than Morgan did, and his leg hurt, perhaps from the explosion. They wobbled past a stairwell, and behind it was a closet, with a couple empty hangers, a mop and a bucket.

Next to the bucket was an opening in the wall, a small rectangular hole. Zvominir squinted at the outline of this shape, which made no sense, an overgrown mouse-hole. There seemed to be a passageway carved into the building, a kind of tunnel, hollowed crudely, as by someone in a panic. Why else would the work seem done by fingernails or forks, desperate and inhuman, as of hands reduced to claws? He had heard the rumors of a Gypsy black market in the sewer, a place of danger and corruption, and, because he was a Swede and not a Gypsy, he had stayed away and so had Morgan. Neither cared for Gypsies. But the volume of voices and gunshots from the rubble-pile grew louder; it sounded like the RedBlacks were clearing wreckage by hand, and forcing the passersby to do it, too. The sound of Mike's obscenities was prominent. Get into the hole, said Zvominir. I'm sick of running, Morgan said, I want to fight, I have to get revenge. Stop posturing, said Zvominir. The swans died because of you.

The Swedes bumped their way into the closet, closed the door behind them, and squeezed through the mousehole in the wall, to a chamber that resembled a crawl-space. They found another hole, this one in the floor. Zvominir peered through the opening, and heard music and voices. He also heard gunshots from the street. He prodded Morgan through the hole, but hardly got himself inside, so awful was his leg-pain.

They stood in what appeared to be a tunnel, and Gypsies were everywhere. Gypsies sat against the walls, stood and played their instruments, danced on wooden platforms, chattered or stared into the blackness. These are things we do between the Earth and sky; Gypsies did them underground, in caves and tunnels dug by us to flee Hungarians, lived in by us during Hungary's occupation. Zvominir led Morgan through the crowd and begged for help, he said his child had been shot, was there a doctor, he couldn't let his child die, though he could hardly walk himself, with how his leg hurt, and soon, it was Morgan hauling Zvominir. They paid a Gypsy boy to take them to a doctor, though Morgan didn't want to pay some fucking guide, and made a bird pick his pocket. Birds appeared to be living underground.

They were led into a kind of open market for stolen surface items, such as furniture, weapons, clothes, shoes and donkeys. How the hell did someone get a bunch of donkeys down here? The floor of the tunnel declined, and the space had the immensity of dreams, like a train station lobby lit by glowing nighttrees as thick as redwoods. This was the biggest single room that either Swede had ever been in. It went on for three square blocks, and surging tides of people cut them off from their guide. Skinny men in suits too tight were pushing mobile metal closet-like contraptions hung with priceless-looking dresses someone must have stolen, and blankets on the floor were lined with nunchuks, Chinese throwing stars, and every kind of kung fu weapon, such as swords that swerved, feathered spears, and shiny tonglike whatsits. Then there were knives, and rows of tubas, and men who dressed as birds and flapped around. The Swedes had no control over them.

The guide, the boy who'd disappeared, re-appeared to say that they didn't look so good. Even Morgan felt too drained to respond.

They staggered past more random object combinations, such as Torahs, Doric columns, chandeliers, dogs, lobsters and Erlenmeyer flasks. At last, they reached a narrow tunnel, where, supposedly, the doctor had his office.

The doctor was said to be busy, so they waited in a queue, amid a grove of nighttrees whose pear-

shaped leaves shone translucent in the darkness.
Nighttrees fed on darkness, and drank of dripping water—and also of the Swede-blood, bashful blood that acted black until the light unmasked it—or whatever they could find, like rugged sub-
terranean iridescent weeds, which is in fact what they were. Jackdaws from the nighttrees hopped off branches onto Morgan, sipped the tears that tumbled from his eyes. The Swedes were concealed beneath a jackdaw blanket wrought by
Zvominir. My swans, Morgan thought, my swans, let me live and I'll avenge you.

Zvominir's vision was failing, for reasons he couldn't quite establish. There was also his excruciating leg-pain to consider, and how it seemed to
blank his consciousness. And Morgan bled and bled, almost to death.

8 Katherine would never be like her mother. Mrs. Giggs was terrified of everything: the birds, the city, Gypsies, strangers, germs, luck, lightning, music; anything could portend tragedy. When Katherine was young, her mother had encouraged her to be curious, but in time, however, Mrs. Giggs grew paranoid, especially when Mike began his RedBlack training, which, to her, somehow seemed to auger doom.

The girl looked out the second-story window of her bedroom at Mike, who had climbed out of his father's carriage and found himself neck-deep in crows. Soldiers rushed him into the house, his face pointing upward as he gasped for breath and tried to break the surface of the birdlake with his lips. He seemed upset as the carriage rode away. She figured Mike had failed again. There was, she knew, a double-standard in the Giggs house, whereby everything she did, good or bad, would be applauded by her father, while Mike was only criticized. The fact that Mike invariably deserved it did not mitigate this injustice, and Katherine couldn't tell if her father had caused Mike's failures, or just responded to them. Mike could have changed this metaphysic by not always fucking up, but that much seemed beyond him.

Katherine stood atop a chair to see out the

window, for birds had clogged her balcony. Standing on the chair was also best for listening to the foyer, where Mike banged past his mother and shuffled up the stairs. The best place to eavesdrop on her parents' bedroom was underneath her bed, not that her parents spoke, though she sometimes heard her mother mothering her father, saying it would be okay, they would do it together. The best place to listen to her father's private study was in the secret liquor closet she was not supposed to know about. Her house was a labyrinth of echoes. She had told her parents of the sounds she had discovered; her father said, Good thing we don't have secrets.

Her father wasn't scared of things. He encouraged Katherine to do anything she wanted. When she said she might want to go to college in Oklahoma, the Judge encouraged her to do it; when she wanted to go downtown alone, he agreed to that, too. She'd heard rumors about his temper and his cruelties, and didn't like his attitude toward Mike, but he was sweet to her, and she was unaware of whatever vague and distant sins he had committed, of which she had so little actual information. Her father was her ally, and she simply didn't know the scope of what she didn't know. To her, he had made the city safe by his stern yet gentle stewardship of history's dreadful forces. This is what she learned in school, and people weren't allowed to tell her otherwise. She didn't know, didn't want to know, and had no opportunity to know.

Katherine stepped off the chair and crossed her forest-feeling bedroom, with its birdlight-dappled floor and chirp-filled air; the kaleidoscopic bird-churn looked incredible. She watched the shadow patterns on her walls, and took a loaf of bread out of her desk drawer. The birds would be hungry, and Katherine would feed them; she'd been doing so all day. She cracked the French doors of her balcony, parrots herding toward the bread. Parrots wriggled through her doors, into the bedroom. She tried to pet their little heads, but they seized the air, landing on her bookshelves or swooping in rainbow-colored streaks. She closed the French doors, but not before more parrots slipped inside. They made her feel uneasy, but she acted like she meant to let them in. Land on my wrist, she said; they didn't; hover above me and sing; they wouldn't; speak in the voice of a girl; they couldn't; make me less lonely, be my companions, hear me when no one else will, read my journal, guard me while I sleep, my room could be your habitat, a safe zone from the bird-purge that everybody wants, Mike says you'll be burned. I want you all to be my pets; she named them Nico, Emma, Edna, Gertrude, Otis, Ursula, Agatha, Agnes, Medea, Quentin, Caddy. Morgan had his swans, and she would have parrots. If only I could get a bird to land on me, she thought. She

74

didn't have a clue what had made the birds consume the city, but she felt the invasion should be
seen as a great opportunity to improve and expand
the city's imagination, civic functions and capacity for love. Her mother seemed dismayed by the
birds in a strangely personal way, and Katherine
didn't understand.

     She kept replaying Morgan's visit in her
mind. She was mesmerized by how he mixed the
ruthless and the vulnerable: his inexplicable, un-
deniable power over birds, the fury of his gaze
and his scrawny tiny weakness—he was skinnier
than her; his shirts were torn and she could see
his ribs!—his eyes, so large and hunted, with their
mix of pride and certain doom. He was like a fugi-
tive in a book, and she would be the moral hero
and protect him, and wash his long and tangled
hair. He somehow seemed more feminine than
her, more slight and needy for protection, and
so much younger than his years, though his soul
was clearly old. He needed help; he needed her
help. She ventured comments to her mother on
his methods with the birds, but her mother called
him lethal. Stay away from him, she said. Katherine countered with a sanctimonious declaration,
called her mother heartless, fascist, racist, and
numerous other awful things. Her mother knew
what Katherine really felt, and Katherine knew
she knew. But Mrs. Giggs embraced the chance
to feel offended, and brooded for days. She was

still upset about it. The years had taught her how to hold a grudge, while Katherine was a novice, whose gifts for battles with her family were still very much in question.

Katherine sat amid her would-be bird-friends in her room. Her mother knocked to ask was she okay. Katherine told her birds to not escape; she wanted to think they had a friendship. *No escape!* they cried, *no escape!* Then she opened her door, and the birds escaped, darting into the hallway and vanishing into the mansion's sky-high upper regions. Their wingbeats echoed everywhere at once. I let the parrots in, Katherine said. Are you crazy, asked her mother. Of course not, they're my pets, my friends, I gave them names.

Her mother didn't stay to hear the names, she spun off down the stairs to track the creatures and expel them. But it was not so easy to expel them. Katherine came downstairs and stood beneath the distant legend of a ceiling while her mother stared up at the dark, ruing how the architecture seemed contrived to hide the birds. How are we supposed to get them out, or even find them? Call out their names, Katherine said. Hey Caddy! Hey Quentin! Come down and meet my mom! Stop talking to them, for God's sake, they're beasts, they could be infected with something. That's what you're really afraid of? An infection? What if the Gypsies are right, and the birds are the souls of the dead? What if one of them is Charlie?

Go to your room, said her mother. Katherine ¹ made an outsized gesture of dissent, and frowned her way back up the stairs, angry and ashamed. Yes, she had erred in letting in the parrots, but she would carry on as though she'd meant it. She ⁵ often caused more damage to her mother than she meant to, and hurt her just because she could.

She went back to her room. Buzzards thrashed against her windows. Climbing her chair in the middle of the room, she listened as her mother ¹⁰ ordered RedBlacks to find the parrots. The chandelier was lowered, lit and raised. Hummingbirds scattered from the light source like bats, parrots were nowhere to be found.

Do you want us to shoot them, asked a ¹⁵ soldier.

Do you want us to shoot! cried the parrots.

Don't shoot in the house, said her mother.

Shoot in the house! cried the parrots. *Squawk! Shoot in the house!* ²⁰

Begging Your Honor's pardon, said a soldier. What should we do if we can't shoot?

Shoot! Beg your pardon! Squawk!

The Gypsies would know what to do, Katherine said from the chair, where she knew her ²⁵ mother heard her.

The Gypsies would know what to do!

You shut your mouth! cried her mother.

Shoot! Shut your mouth! Shoot inside the house! Shout your mouth! ³⁰

Bootsteps and wingbeats rustled in her ears as soldiers raced around the house. *Charlie! Charlie!*

Now she couldn't tell the birds or soldier's feet apart; sound of frantic gunmen merged with birds. Her mother cried out, Mike! Don't shoot! Gun blasts crashed the silence of Katherine's bird-tuned ears. Her brother was shooting up the house, and crying, Die, bird, die! The noise made her ears ring.

The shooting stopped, all of a sudden. What the hell is going on here, asked her father, who must have just come home. Mike began to say that Katherine let parrots into the house, but the Judge cut him off, demanded the gun, and screamed at Mike to go up to his room. She had never heard her father yell like that. What had Mike done to provoke it?

Mike's jackboots clopped up the stairs, and out of echo. Next, her father asked her mother what had happened. She confirmed Mike's asser- tion: Katherine let the parrots in, and now they were screaming. Scapegoat me, why don't you, Katherine said.

Scapegoat!

Who was that, asked the Judge. The parrots, said his wife.

Fan out, he told his RedBlacks, and shoot them on sight. No one bothered telling him this strategy had already failed. He didn't like to be corrected; he considered it unpatriotic. Instead, the soldiers kept on hurrying around, chasing voices and trying to look busy.

Shoot Charlie on sight!

Katherine left her room and came downstairs to find her parents standing side-by-side in the foyer. Above them, parrots engaged in what could only be described as a Charlie screaming contest. Her father had an automatic rifle in his hands, and peered through the sights into the darkness of the house. He looked miserable, though he softened when he saw Katherine. Mrs. Giggs did not do likewise.

Chasing the parrots doesn't work, Katherine said. Her father was about to ask what, in her wisdom, she would recommend, but a chicken wandered in, with hay in its beak. It made itself at home on the rug.

You gotta be kidding me, said the Judge. Mrs. Giggs started crying. Zvominir and Morgan could get rid of them, said Katherine, who described how the Swedes had lifted the birds from the yard. You didn't tell me that, the Judge said to his wife. Chickens with hay in their beaks had formed a parade. I'm sure all you have to do is ask them to come back, Katherine said.

9 Morgan lay recuperating on a cot, and his father lay nearby. According to the doctor, the bullet which had grazed Morgan's ribs had passed first through Zvominir's leg, and ricocheted off the tibia, which it cracked. Morgan had a bandage on his side where his wound had been disinfected, and he required no more treatment, but Zvominir's bloodgushing bullet-tunneled thigh needed cauterizing, a process accomplished with a glowing hot poker. Zvominir would henceforth have a limp. He also got a better bandage on his thumb.

Morgan felt embarrassed to be hiding underground instead of fighting on the surface, but he also felt remorse for the suffering of his father, who had cried out in agony. The boy was contrite; he had cried, and tried to hide his tears, and covered up his shame by picking fights. He told his father not to scream, it sounded weak, and the doctor tired of listening to them fight, and ordered the boy to take a puff of his medicinal cigarette, which left his consciousness transformed.

Light white as nighttrees beamed through gaps in the streets overhead. He feared for the birds that surrounded him, crept to him, huddled to his body like a feather-shroud. He wondered how they'd found him here; did birds live underground? Did they glide through sewer-grates or dive into a chimney? Curlews and kestrels camouflaged his body, he saw nothing through their feathers, for the birds that disappeared him; they were gathered by his father, whose gifts were greater than his own, so he could merely beg. Crowd me not, sweet fools, he thought, for I am not your savior, I can only herd you, make patterns in the sky with you, be ruled by me and leave these catacombs forever, obey me as a pilgrim would a brass god poured by humans. Fly off from this dank and narrow cellar of the earth! Birds who follow me are slaughtered. Leave this catacomb of pearly nighttrees bleached in darkness, see-through trees with blurry leaves that drip their sap above the Gypsy heads and drink the sewer water in this tunnel. Escape before you're murdered, like my swans.

Still associative with smoke, the boy lay motionless and hungry, and wondered when he'd eat. If he'd been at home, he could've foraged through dumpsters for leftovers. Did the café exist anymore? RedBlacks had probably gone looking for him there, it had probably been destroyed. He didn't know that RedBlacks hardly went into the ghetto, and felt a strange affection for his old home and the neighborhood, which he'd hated until now. Now that it was probably in flames, he missed it, and regretted that he hadn't said goodbye, or at least helped finish it off in some way, so

pure was his contempt for this building where the
walls seemed to shudder with the voices of people
who cried out in their sleep, where the well had
brown water, and where pigeons roosted on the
roof, though he actually liked the pigeons: filthy,
ratlike creatures who lived anywhere, on anything, a gift he ruefully admired.

He gazed through his birdshroud at his father, who looked more scared than ever, sitting
on his cot and poking at the bandage on his leg.
The medicinal cigarette was wearing off.

You don't how lucky we are, said his father,
but Morgan thought, I don't feel lucky.

10 Soon, RedBlacks occupied the tunnel. Gypsies were kicked and insulted, handcuffed and tagged with numbers, dragged away for questioning and dumped back in their puddles, though some would be killed, as with the doctor who had treated the Swedes. The soldiers shot the nighttrees, spattering the floor with silver blood and scaring off the birds. Best you should scatter for good, Morgan thought; my swans, I betrayed you, it's my fault you're dead, my fault and the RedBlacks, and I'll punish them for you. He would aim his rage at the world, or at least he would try.

RedBlacks were plowing at pace through the Gypsies. Morgan watched as soldiers plucked a Gypsy from her loom, and dragged her down the tunnel, out of sight. I'm not going to wait for us to die, said his father. I'm going to get us out of here.

Zvominir and Morgan crept off into darkness, stepping over Gypsies who rocked in place and wept, huddled near fires or tried to mend their clothes, played their mournful, ancient-seeming music, their instruments of brass too old to shine, their faces deeply wrinkled, almost cracked. We're nothing more than rats, Morgan thought.

A pair of RedBlacks caught the Swedes from

behind, demanding to know where they were going. Nowhere in particular, said Zvominir, and shoved his son behind him, to protect him.

The shorter of the RedBlacks raised his lantern, and lit up all their faces. Morgan recognized the soldiers, and they recognized him, too; they grinned, pleasantly surprised. These were the friends of Mike Giggs. They had chased him through the streets.

Just who we were looking for, the tall one said, beaming. Morgan tried to wriggle from his father's protection, and he punched at the soldier, but the soldiers whacked his face with their gunbutts, and kicked out his feet. Zvominir did his best to intervene; Fuck off, dad, they said, and hit him, too. Zvominir crawled across the body of his son and pleaded as kicks struck his ribs, and his son's, and their wounds bled again.

A cluster of older, age-appropriate RedBlacks arrived to inspect the fallen Swedes, and chided their inquisitors for beating them. The torturers complained they'd only started having fun. Let us kill them, they begged. Fuck off back to your treehouse, said the grownups, The Judge is looking for them.

The younger RedBlacks stood their ground: the orders said to kill them, and that's what they were going to do, when they'd finished having fun. The grownups said the mission of this underground endeavor had been changed, the Gypsies were now to be delivered to the surface, not killed outright. Hand them over, they said. The soldier boys looked wistfully at Morgan, splattered him with phlegm, withdrew into the shadows, and swore to get him next time.

Thank you, said Zvominir, who stood. You are kind.

The soldiers whacked him in the face with their gun-butts. The Swede fell again.

Zvominir wobblingly stood and lifted Morgan, and tried to gimp along with the soldiers as they marched through the tunnel. His face felt strange and swollen, and he almost couldn't see. The pain was fierce, but felt like it belonged to something else, some other ruined body which had taken over his. Morgan could hardly believe he wasn't dead, and felt exasperated, yet thankful. The tunnel curved and wound in brutal progress through the stone, and Gypsies turned their faces from the soldiers in fear. Morgan both blamed the Gypsies for their caution and didn't, but mostly, he blamed them. It wouldn't be so hard for all these people to hurl themselves at two or three RedBlacks. What stopped them?

They turned another corner, and found a coffin-sized hole where the tunnel had collapsed, where rubble made a black and sooty hill up to the surface, sunlight blasting through the maw, stabbing into Morgan's eyes like shards, and all the nearby nighttrees dead and shriveled. Squint-

ing, he scrambled to the surface, his father stag-
gering behind him. It took a while for Morgan's
eyes to function in the sunlight, but slowly, he saw
it wasn't sunlight. It was glowing grayish smog.
Morgan remembered the blue of the countryside
sky, near the Judge's estate. He wanted to see it
again.

He was in a square which resembled the
Piazza, but this one had no steps, only isolated
sculptures of yellow, sandy stone he didn't recognize, and through a row of arches was the river.
He hadn't known that there was water near the
city; the still and greenish surface mesmerized
him. Seagulls afloat on the water started screeching, surging toward Swedes, and vultures, too,
but Morgan kept them at a distance. The Bird Boy
didn't want the birds getting hurt. He thought, at
least you guys should live.

RedBlacks in the square closed ranks around
the Swedes.

The Bird Man and his son were shoved to
their knees. Rifles were pressed to their heads.
When Zvominir tried protecting Morgan, soldiers
held him to the ground. A RedBlack officer approached, with a scroll in his hand. Do you have
to fucking read some declaration before you kill
us, Morgan said. Bureaucratic pussies. The officer
with the scroll kicked the boy in the ribs. Then he
read an edict from the Judge, which ordered the
Swedes to work as bird-custodians, and control

the bird-invasion, to regulate the creatures as one
would any pest. You'll be paid a modest sum. The
Judge changed his mind, for whatever reason. It's
your lucky day.

You people killed my swans, Morgan said.
Why should I help you? Shut the hell up, said his
father. We know, said the officer, that the Gypsies are people just like us, or almost, and that
you'd recognize a decent offer, and won't spurn
a chance to save yourselves, especially since we
wouldn't even make it if our own lives weren't in
ruins due to birds.

We're nothing like you, Morgan said, we're
Swedes, sobs ruining his words. He was crying
now and furious with himself, furious at the father who had womaned him with tears, as vengeance had manned him with rage.

Zvominir was handed a pen, and signed the
contract while still prone on the ground, the gun
still at his head. Have mercy on us, he said. Where
do I get to sign, asked the boy. You don't, said the
officer. You're too young. Morgan thought, when I
grow up, I'll avenge these never-ending disgraces.
Vultures were crying out all over the square, like
black and tortured desperate swans. Unyouth me
here, he prayed, and take away my weakness, give
me influence and strength. I swear that you will
be avenged.

It's a deal, said the officer. Let them go.
RedBlack doctors examined the Swedes,

and admitted that the Gypsy who had treated them in the tunnel had done a perfect job. They regretted his murder. Plates of meat and vegetables, potatoes, bread and fruit were brought out to the Swedes, which Zvominir carried through the arches to the river, where he and Morgan sat along the wall. After he had eaten, Morgan tossed chunks of bread to the seagulls. It turned out that the river was no river, but a dried-up riverbed of green waving reeds and skipping frogs, together with a zillion venus flytraps, their lashes blinking flirty death with languor. The seagulls, as it happened, were mostly white pigeons. Morgan felt a little disappointed, but cheered himself by ordering another plate from soldiers who'd been ordered to protect him from other soldiers.

This meat is well done, Morgan said. Teach your so-called chefs not to vandalize a steak with overcooking. The soldiers stomped off, looking angry; they'd been made to serve a Gypsy, or whatever the hell he was. And bring some more bread, he called, The birds get hungry, too. And tuck in your shirt, you're an affront to psychopaths.

We could get killed, said his father. Are you crazy?

Morgan took his steak knife and tied it to his ankle with a shred of his torn-up shirt, concealing it with his pant-leg. No one's going to kill us, he said. These fuckers need us. And once we've saved the birds, I'll kill the Judge myself.

Viva la Muerte!

11 Morgan worked all day to rid the city of its birds, a process called de-birding. In de-birding, Zvominir and Morgan roamed the city and the suburbs, surrounded by RedBlacks, and banished flocks of birds from all the neighborhoods. Birds which left the city on Sunday would fly back by Wednesday, called back, we assume, by whatever force had called them in the first place. The Swedes worked every day, and rode a flatbed trailer pulled by horses. Zvominir was businesslike, solicitous of mercy, and flattered RedBlack constituents and sympathizers. Anyone who liked the Judge would be respected by the Bird Man, and he worked in the suburbs, where people could trust him, more or less, or at least trust that he feared them. He behaved in reassuring, sycophantic ways, and minimized his limp.

But Morgan, who suburban grownups feared—though their children by now idolized the Bird Boy for his power and rebellious reputation—only worked the city. The Judge didn't want the Gypsy population inflamed by the Bird Boy, who was known to be cantankerous, but he couldn't have Morgan in the suburbs either, where his rage could not be trusted. And so he worked the ghetto, escorted by RedBlacks, who kept track of all he did and said. Despite the orders of the soldiers, he always made a birdshow of de-birding.

After seven weeks of regular de-birding, the birdlakes of the city and especially the suburbs had been drained almost completely, and life returned to something nearly normal. We could see our lawns again, our land had been reclaimed, our lives restored, almost, but for memories of war or of loss—the birds had dredged these up from our forgetting.

Morgan de-birded in the day, and did his birdshow at night, at the bottom of the Steps, and for money. Word of mouth had led to vast expansions of his audience. All the city's children came to watch him, or wanted to, and so did the adults, mainly Gypsies, who flocked to see him without shame; we could hardly do the same, and so came camouflaged as chaperones. We had to see him too, though none of us confessed to this desire.

Everyone knew the Swedes by now. Half the city loved them, the other half hated them, but together, we all feared their power. They were either targeted by spite and flying vegetables, or deluged by awe. Their RedBlack escorts didn't trust them, and the people whose homes they de-birded held them liable for the birds. How could we be blamed for wondering if Zvominir and Morgan hadn't cursed us? The bird-show audience, meanwhile, loved them utterly, the rich and poor and all the in-the-middle folks who complicate this binary, who gathered on the Steps and watched, side-by-side, huddling on the gold stones of the Square and clogging up the streets of the city for an hour every night. The hats the Swedes passed around were overfilled with bills; the crowd would shake the stones of the Square with their approval.

Birdshows were generally narrative, and featured a bird-made Morgan being chased through the streets by a soldier who was torn to bits by swans, though the swans were made of pigeons, and the soldier of flesh-colored plovers, his uniform of cardinals and crows. Swans would also be pursued through ghetto canyons by flying tigers made of orioles. These were his intentions for the birdshows, at any rate, but Zvominir would censor when the images betrayed but a hint of dangerous content, obscuring Morgan's work with birdclouds, or worse, laughing babies made of birds. The audience found these touches psychedelic, and weren't pacified so much as confused, so their passion turned to mumbles. The elder's power over birds was superior, and Morgan couldn't stop his father from suppressing the transgressive. It infuriated him.

Zvominir de-birded at the Giggs house almost every day, which seemed to be the capital of birds. Maybe they were cursed, but what distinguished them from everybody else? Wasn't everybody cursed? Was the Giggs' curse worse? He saw that Mrs. Giggs only left her bedroom to accompany Katherine, or maintain her gardens, or do housework in a frantic, almost miserable way, crumpling the bed sheets and bleaching colored clothes, cooking things that nobody would eat, though her servants seemed to undo what she did, or rather, she undid what they did. She had also banned her daughter from the birdshows. Her father had said that she could go, but in practice, her mother still held sway. It was the red tape of their family. Zvominir's visits were the only contact Katherine could have with the Swedes.

Katherine followed Zvominir around, wanting to be friendly with the birds, and pet their pretty feathers. Zvominir told her not to touch them, it ruined their scent, to just be satisfied with looking, for human love devoured them, though the Swedes left no scent, which was odd, because they stank. The voice of Katherine's mother crashed down from the windows, telling her to leave him alone, and keep her mind off birds, but she ignored her mother's orders. She wanted to assist the birds somehow, the goslings and baby hawks and eagles, and the toucans. Zvominir liked her curiosity, but feared how it stoked her mother's temper.

Katherine adored the parrots she had let into the house, but Mrs. Giggs insisted they be banished, so the Giggs girl begged Zvominir to hide them. She loved the talking birds, even if they shouted Charlie's name. She could teach them new words, she insisted, and said that fate deprived them of a land, that man had marooned them in a world that was awful, and what should they do but resent it, and insult their oppressors? We can rehabilitate the parrots, she said. Please don't send them out to die, I don't have any friends but them, them and you.

Katherine was frequently alone. Her mother could be found in the garden, pulling weeds or rearranging furniture in a *feng shui* of sabotage, so everyone would trip or feel disoriented, or sitting by herself in her bedroom. Mike spent his days on the prowl with his troop-friends, and the Judge was busy working. No one spoke to Katherine but Zvominir and the parrots, and, truth be told, she gave Zvominir the only normal conversation he would have all day. She was a sweet and good-natured child, unlike his own son, and Zvominir liked pretending she was his. He'd grown weary of Morgan's tantrums, which had not diminished with success. The boy liked to boast he was *Keeping It Real*, which seemed to mean that he would go on being stupid, no matter his good fortune. So Katherine came as a relief, and Zvominir would help her, if he could.

He tried to hide the birds in distant regions of the house, begged them to be quiet and discreet, scared he'd be punished and hating that he'd put himself and Morgan at risk by flouting orders, but wanting so to please pleading Katherine, whose good nature brought him joy. The birds would

still erupt, mocking Mrs. Giggs by crying, *Charlie!*
Shoot the fucker! Finally, the Judge sent a note
to the Swede, which explained that if the parrots
spoke again, he and Morgan would be killed. *I*
don't have time to threaten you in person, wrote   5
the Judge, *so busy am I threatening others. I*
would merely remind you that I'm politically ex-
ploiting you, so don't make your murder look ad-
vantageous to me. Think of me as the only thing
standing between you and a death achieved by   10
almost primeval means, with cave man-era cut-
ting tools and so forth.

   Thus did Zvominir make his desperate stab
at removal, though he knew the tidelike rhythm of
migration guaranteed the parrots would be back.   15
He led them from the house just after dawn, and
they cried for joy and mischief in the sun, calling:
Shoot the fucker! Mike is going crazy! Whore of
shit! He rode a yellow horse to the border, where
thirty-seven parrots—they'd had babies; baby   20
parrots!; soft-beaked and blind and drowsing
in a nest atop his head, their mothers standing
guard on his horse as their fathers flew above, not
talking, now worried—thirty-seven parrots were
abandoned near Angola, spirits bleak and feath-   25
ers fading grayly in the darkness—no color without light—the day had curdled into dusk, and yet
it was only noon; birds were immigrating back.
Katherine's parrots were deserted, lonesome and
saying *We blame you for Charlie.*   30

12 Morgan and Zvominir stood by the fountains and waited to start the bird-show. Zvominir only allowed them because they made money. He never asked the crowd to pay, but the audience stuffed bills into hats and gave them to the Swedes, which, even after soldiers dipped their beaks into these sums, the Bird Man and his son still had enough for food.

Jane, Morgan's pretty, dangerous-looking girlfriend, stood nearby, as did Billy, her tall and sloppy brother. There was hardly any room for them to move, with the crowds and the RedBlacks and the Gypsies playing *ska* and selling bird food. Officers forced their way to Zvominir, and handed him commandments. He and the RedBlacks had a policy of circumventing Morgan, and they passed notes between each other, orders which invariably had him as their subject. Already, they'd admonished him to not engage his customers, to not respond to taunts, or even compliments. Each of these instructions had been given first to his father, and enforced by the soldiers who escorted Morgan everywhere he went, as if they walked him like a doggie.

Is that about me, Morgan asked.

Of course it is, said a RedBlack, who read the sheet aloud, in front of everyone, to Zvominir's

horror. He didn't want his son provoked in public, but RedBlacks loved to push his buttons. That
way, Zvominir figured, they'd have plausible deni-
ability when they shot him forty times. *He got angry! What were we supposed to do?* It made the
Bird Man sick; threats to Morgan multiplied with
every passing moment. Further: because these
notes would pit the boy against him, he had no
way to calm Morgan down. The power over birds
had not exactly unified them.

The sheet explained that birdshows should
henceforth be positive, life-affirming, and most of
all, Judge-affirming. Everyone is happy, went the
orders, and birdshows should augment our happiness, and not give anyone ideas. Gloom can be
contagious. Yes, the note belittled Morgan, and
the audience, and human beings in general, and
minimized our quarry as sentient beings, etc, but
we would like to state for the record that we do
not disagree with it.

In any case, the birdshow. Morgan tried to
make some violent images, but Zvominir formed
the birds into a giant orb, and curled a second
layer of birds around the first. The orbs spun in
opposite directions, and were lit up by the sun,
which happened to be setting between buildings.
The whole construction was a kind of magic lamp,
and cast a shadow pattern on the audience. The
outer level blotted out the inner as a story, but
embellished it as a tissue of sensations. We could

not have cheered any louder, but Morgan felt betrayed. The audience didn't know the birdshow wasn't his. Morgan called his father a sellout, and ran off with Jane and Billy.

I'm trying to save you, Zvominir cried, then he turned to the RedBlacks charged with the care of Morgan and said, Chase him. The RedBlacks shrugged, lazy, drunk and busy playing poker, while Zvominir tore off for his son. We are master killers, thought the RedBlacks. Why should we follow these con men through the city? We aren't even bodyguards, we're escorts. Anus. This job is demeaning.

Morgan ran through the streets with Jane and Billy, while RedBlacks and Zvominir huffed and puffed behind them, asking bystanders if they'd seen the Bird Boy. RedBlacks we answered; his father we laughed at, or even ignored, it was fun to watch him suffer; we considered him the artist of our bird-pain, and plus his limp was creepy, no matter how much he effaced it.

That which Zvominir had dreaded came to pass. Sitting in the square, at the head of a long table covered with fruit and various liquors, was Mike Giggs, surrounded by his RedBlacks, friends and girls, and also the band he'd corralled at the Steps, who played their festive Gypsy *ska*. Morgan stood across from them.

13

Goaded by Jane, Morgan dug a rock from the cobblestone square and gunned it at Mike. The rock flew wide and smashed a carafe, red wine and glass drenching bystander girls, making them scream, their dresses stained and ruined. Mike ducked under the table, thinking he'd been shot at, and the band came to a halt.

Bitch, Morgan said. Rich bitch, Jane called.

Mike stood, relieved. Oh, he said, it's you, I thought it was someone dangerous. I am dangerous, Morgan said. Yeah right, pin-dick, I've been meaning to kill you for weeks, you're lucky I'm so, um, what's that word my dad used?

Languid, said a RedBlack.

Yeah, languid. From getting laid all day, like.

Morgan's steak knife pressed against his leg, and he wanted to use it.

Mike told his bodyguards to shoot him. He assumed the birds had come to herald his heroic stage, to facilitate his destiny of coolness, and he didn't like the Bird Boy stealing his thunder. The RedBlacks explained they weren't allowed to shoot the Bird Boy or his father. What the hell are you talking about, Mike said, and repeated his order. The RedBlacks continued that the Swedes were off-limits where violence was concerned, and

99

were to be protected at all times, and that the city, and his father's regime, required their powers, no matter how odious they seemed. You're letting him throw rocks at us, Mike said, ducking as more cobblestones zoomed in, hitting other girls.

Zvominir arrived, seized Morgan by the collar, and ordered him to not provoke Mike. Jane shook her head in disgust, and called Zvominir a Judas. The Swede berated Morgan's bodyguards, and too many people had gathered between Mike and Morgan for anyone to shoot. The square returned to drunken chaos. Mike stood on the banquet table, screaming his intention to kill Morgan, and the band began to play again, on orders from the guards, who went back to getting drunk.

We're going home now, said Zvominir, shoving Morgan through the crowd, and although the boy pretended he was angry—and, in many ways, he was—he also felt thrilled to go back to the storefront, because he had food there. Business was so good they had leftovers now; Morgan ate five meals a day.

Father and son returned to the storefront in silence, where Zvominir rinsed plates in the kitchen, and Morgan gorged on leftovers. Jane says the Judge is cursed by the birds, Morgan said. Everyone has birds, Zvominir said, Since when do strangers tell you what the birds mean? She also say birds are my art, and my fate, I shouldn't let them be censored. Zvominir did not respond. He used to think his son would get mature by grow- ing up, but his hope was disappearing.

In the morning, before his lazy Morgan woke, Zvominir found the RedBlack officer whose job it was to bodyguard the boy. This RedBlack, Noah, was a furry-necked and grumpy stumpish little man whose bald head dripped with sweat, and who sneered from the corner of his mouth instead of speaking. What the fuck do you want shitface, was the greeting Zvominir received.

He offered Noah extra money to follow Morgan, to keep him out of trouble and protect him. Noah smirked, incredulous, and boasted to the other gathered RedBlacks of Zvominir's offer. I'm serious, said the Bird Man, I have money. He produced a wad of bills from his pocket, which he hoped would make him look impressive. It was almost everything he had, this stack of bills; it was three hundred dollars. He didn't know where he would get the rest.

He pleaded with Noah, and felt he didn't have a choice. Safeguard my boy, he begged. Please. Sure, Noah said. I'll take your money.

14

Jane the Gypsy, aged twenty, lived in Morgan's neighborhood, and first approached him at a block party, not long after he'd been hired by the Judge. No matter the attention he'd received from girls while de-birding or at birdshows, he had no real experience with them. Girls would stare in awe, but never spoke, and how would he have answered if they did, he was shy, so he tried acting tough. It worked, insofar as girls were scared, which meant it ultimately didn't work. So, there he was, amid the hordes of Gypsy teens, standing by himself, looking mean and feeling lonely, too afraid to talk and too self-conscious to go back to his apartment. He stood against a lamppost, sipping nothing from an empty cup he felt too nervous to re-fill. Jane, with her swooping, wolfish nose, long and rusty-colored hair, and giant eyes that parsed him like a code, walked right up and started talking. She was tall, sincere, and she looked enviously happy, and had a gravitas that somehow seemed beyond him. Not only did he lust for her: he admired her.

Morgan had approximated something of a swagger, and used it to impress her. In lieu of actually talking, which he pretended to eschew on the grounds it was for suckers, he did bird-tricks. He made bluebirds pour down off the rooftop of

her building and plash into a pigeon-spume, then
he led her through a forest, the trunks of choughs
and sparrows, the canopy of cockatiels, with cardinals as the fruit. Can you do fire, she asked. He
found the birds for fire, and built her an inferno.
Morgan left no tricks undone, conserved no power; he was hasty to be loved. It's unbelievable, she
said, fairly gasping. He shrugged; he had practiced looking nonchalant.

   Morgan talked about his swans, of how he
loved them, and the awful way they'd died, though
he omitted that his temper played a part in the
equation of their death, and so felt that he'd de-
ceived her, somehow. His father's version of the
swans would be different, but Jane was not his
father, and he could craft his own identity with
her. I want to take the RedBlacks down, he said,
and certainly believed it in his heart, wherever
that was, but he only claimed it now because Jane
craved to hear it. He figured it was fine to use his
own biography and powers as tools for seduction.
What good were they otherwise? Life owes me, he
thought.

   Jane had a brother named Billy, age fifteen,
tall and looming, like a tree about to topple, his
brown hair like an awning, overhanging, and with
floppy lips to match. His hands and feet were
clownish; he was like a puppy yet to grow into
his limbs. Jane hoped he never did. He looked so
goofy he could only be sincere. Where he sham-

bled, she was graceful; where her features were distinct but composed, his dangled off his face, as if he was her hastily assembled simulacrum, a dodo to her swan. Jane adored her younger brother, her only living relative, her ward and her devoted best friend; lesser in intelligence, perhaps, but great in loyalty and sweetness, and those were all that mattered. With Morgan, as with Jane, he was credulous and eager.

Together, they had learned to steal their food, dodged the RedBlacks all their lives, and memorized the tunnels by the time she was twelve and he was seven. They'd been chased by RedBlacks from a dozen different buildings where they'd squatted; their fellow squatters had been beaten. Getting whaled on by the RedBlacks was considered a right of passage by the Gypsies, but Jane swore such a thing would never happen to her brother, and they lived now underground, where nobody could find them. They stole everything they needed, and had never done a day of so-called honest work. Life for Gypsies was unjust, she said, and she and Billy would never be exploited, though neither would they fight, they were pacifists, or Jane was a pacifist, and Billy did what he was told. Billy said that Jane excelled at breaking into buildings through the tunnels, and any kind of criminal pursuit that harmed only institutions, as opposed to human bodies. He was massive on the issue of her excellence at crime, her devotion to its arts, her skill at finding holes in any building that connected to the tunnels. Her ideas were a muddle, but Morgan didn't care. It was great having friends.

The first time Morgan broke into a store with them, Billy tried to enter first, but Jane wouldn't let him; Get behind me, she said, You know the rule, don't show off for Morgan. She didn't want her brother getting caught, there might be a security guard in there. How she would have dealt with this imaginary guard she didn't say, but she wouldn't have her brother implicated.

The entrance was a narrow filthy hole cut through the concrete, like all the other spider holes, and led up from the tunnels to a closet. Morgan had to wedge himself in place many feet above the tunnel, and he found he hated heights. Jane greased the closet's sliding doors with oil, and opened them in silence. She was serious and nimble; her skills were forged from practice and intelligence, as opposed to Morgan's powers, which had come to him from nowhere. The contrast intrigued him: here was someone who had earned things. Morgan hadn't cared who went first into the store, until he actually reached the hole, at which point he felt terrified, and saw that Billy, who might well be foolish, still was brave. Jane disappeared into the world beyond the closet, and returned a moment later, to report the coast was clear.

As Morgan came up through the closet, which he found was full of uniforms—blue shirts and matching pants—he frisked the pockets for cash, but Jane said, Don't, we don't rob employees, this is the janitor's changing room, some of them may be Gypsies. Indeed, righteous crime was Jane's idea of citizenship. She had rules and principles and clauses, and every kind of nuance. She never took more than she needed to survive, or stole anything expensive—fancy clothes, for example—for those would make them look suspicious on the street, and might draw the eye of RedBlacks, and plus, she and Billy weren't vulgar, they had no need for ostentation, they had anti-RedBlack values. Morgan meekly put a twenty-dollar bill back in the pocket where he'd found it. He supposed he agreed with Jane's ideas, but they weren't so fun to live by. Nonetheless, her upstanding jokeless rectitude only added to her sexual allure. He liked that she was proper in her outlaw way; a little bit stuck-up.

What he saw of this "department store" was different than the tunnel in almost every way, and yet they lay atop each other. Where the tunnels were a labyrinth, the store was a grid; a prison, where the tunnels were a mystery. The tunnels were grimy and hopeless; the store was white and disinfected, angularly vicious, while the tunnels were indifferent in their roundness. Department stores sold everything expensive and new;

THE AVIAN GOSPELS

the tunnels had it broken, cheap and stolen. Presumably the shoppers never thought about the tunnels, and tunnel-dwellers seemed to lack the agency to storm the store above. We already have established the unhappiness of those who lived below, but Morgan found it too clean for his taste here, too reflective even in the halflight; lonely and so ruthless for its hoarding of desire. If Zvominir could see the treasures hidden here, the furniture and clothes and all the shoes and the flawless kitchen tables, he would give away his soul.

Jane left Morgan and her brother in the office of the manager, and went to rob the registers, while Billy instructed Morgan how to jimmy open safes, a skill he'd learned from Jane, who'd taught herself by stealing books on criminology from various city libraries. She hoped to someday graduate to white collar crime, to bilk a bank of fortunes, own some buildings of her own, and charge outrageous rent, launder money through her real estate. She was ambitious. Ambition could be hot. And yet, here was Morgan, stuck with Billy, while Jane's ambition interfered with Morgan's wish for sex. You have to listen, Billy said, kneeling by the safe and twirling on the knob, with fingers that resembled lobster legs, for any kind of click, you have to be quiet, shhh, shhh, almost. Yet, where Billy'd ordered Morgan not to speak—politely, of course—he couldn't stop himself from asking flattering questions, like, Aren't you frightened when they beat you, is it cool to be the savior of the dead, and was it fun to beat up Mike Giggs in his house?

Morgan could be prone to perpetuating factual distortions.

The office had an ugly tile ceiling, a dirty-looking floor of grayblack speckles, and a desk with framed pictures of a family whose patriarch just might be canned tomorrow, for how easy it had been to rob his store. This happy family man with his grin seemed to painlessly accept the bursting double-neck he had acquired, the hair he'd lost, and how his body had essentially gone to shit. Billy cracked the safe. Say what you will about his face and geek demeanor, he could simultaneously speak and do his job, he was fifty times the man of action Morgan was, and wasn't pacing by the door, rubbing his hands in fear he'd be arrested. If Morgan's reputation as a badass hadn't blinded Billy, the Bird Boy would've looked as anxious as he felt. What if he got caught? His taste for getting beaten up was disappearing.

And where the hell was Jane? Billy searched the desk for some kind of payroll records, but Morgan didn't care; he wanted Jane, and left the office to go look for her. But finding Jane in the vast department store was not so easy. For one thing, it sold absolutely every single thing he could imagine: cutlery, plates, brooms, mops, mirrors, toys, and something called "patio furniture," which seemed like regular furniture, if white. He was lost, he couldn't see the registers, and roamed forlorn among the shelves, alone and horny. Instead of finding Jane, he found that sexual desire was linked to sadness.

When he finally climbed atop a shelf to get a bird's eye view, he could see the Earth's curve. Fuck it, he thought. He yelled, Jane! That got her attention; she came running from a region of the store he thought he'd checked, but it seemed that he was careless, and Jane said Shut up, someone could hear. I thought you had that covered, he said, and gestured at a nearby field of beds.

His words were, Look at all those beds!

Jane resisted blushingly. She was tall and beautiful and complex, stately and substantial, if not exactly thin; composed and dignified and dire; she had presence and power, but most of all, purpose. It was his cause to make her laugh when she was working, to forget her job and kiss him; he set about the task of his irreverence, and found that she could be seduced, that she loved joy as much as anyone. You have all your rules, he said, and I have your body. Give me a break, she said, does that line really work? It did this time, Morgan said. They used a bed to roll around on, more in earnest imitation of what might occur in beds, but hey, it was a start. Then they tried another bed. Later, she apologized to Billy, who claimed he hadn't felt left out; he'd catalogued the pay stubs in the office, and even stole a pair of hi-top shoes for Morgan on the sly.

Billy liked to steal for Morgan. While Jane was out reconnoitering, he taught Morgan how to pick a pocket, or rob a store in daylight. After, they'd buy liquor with the spoils, and find the best Gypsy bands. They spent more time together than Morgan did with Jane.

One day, Jane and Morgan walked on the surface to see a *ska* band she had heard about. She was often nervous when she wasn't underground, but there didn't seem to be a military presence in this neighborhood, and Morgan didn't sense the usual tension. Trees had leaves on their branches, not just plastic bags, and children didn't look unhappy; they didn't have that distance in their eyes, that futility. Morgan actually relaxed.

But the band, when they found it in the street, had some RedBlacks in their audience. The soldiers stood in front and slammed each other to the rhythm, and Jane insisted that they leave, but then she saw her brother dancing, too, near the stage, among the soldiers and undaunted.

What the hell is he doing, she said.

The audience had about a dozen Gypsies, and everyone appeared to be getting along, but Jane yanked Billy from the crowd and marched him into a bodega, to a closet and underground, into a tunnel filled with windowpanes.

I told you, she said, yelling, never ever get

close to soldiers. Are you stupid?

Billy looked surprised and embarrassed, but not as angry as Morgan expected. He didn't seem to know he had the right to lose his temper and assert himself. We were only dancing, he said, meekly.

I don't care, said Jane. They're not your friends, they're dangerous. You don't just dance around with RedBlacks.

It's not like they were beating anyone up. They were nice. It was normal.

She grabbed his collar and pushed him against the wall. Morgan had never seen her half this angry. She had turned maroon. It's never normal with them, she said. They're not even human. They blackmail people like us, they kill us for no reason. You have to be more careful.

She stalked off down the tunnel. Billy seemed ashamed, and wouldn't look at Morgan. The Bird Boy also felt uncomfortable, and feared he'd sound unserious and weak if he offered consolation. Better to let Billy hate the RedBlacks than intervene ambiguously and somehow end up looking bad. They shuffled off after Jane.

Later that night, as Billy, Jane and Morgan trekked beneath the ground, they came to an arena where Gypsies prayed to birds, a massive domelike cavern called a Megachurch. Bearded men in bird-suits sang devotional rock-steady on a stage, and did what looked like rapid deep-knee bends accompanied by leaps, an exercise that rippled through the crowd, but all the deep-knee-bender-leapers looked decrepit, they were old, and grunted through excruciating prayers. Others prayed by whacking their own bodies with sacramental whips lined with bird-beaks, or chirping at the roof. Chirpers let the spirit of the bird god take possession of their bodies; it used their mouths to speak its language, though perhaps without the eloquence of birds, for men are different than Philomela. Others rolled upon the ground and groaned, spittle hopping from their mouths, and though it wasn't prayer, they actually had seizures, no one knew the difference.

Fanatics wearing black balaclavas made their Molotov Cocktails where everyone could see—their workshop like a lemonade stand—hoping to evangelize the tunnels to rebellion, as they had been evangelized by Mike's Bazooka Massacre, as they'd named it. The appeal was minimal, and Jane agreed with almost all the Gypsies: let's draw no attention to ourselves; let's have some peace and not start trouble. Thus did tunnel rebels fail to gain coherence. Every now and then, they set off an explosion, but their history was a slapdash of failures.

Pickpockets dressed like birds came phony-flying through the crowd, bashing into worshippers, absconding with their money. It made Jane sick. Then there were the normal-looking Gypsies, mostly teens, who smoked a plant they'd rolled into a cigarette—the same plant Morgan smoked in the tunnel, after the swan-atrocity—which added languor to their vigor of their youth, and made them lazy, and prone to wild laughter, though nothing Morgan saw was very funny. Vulnerable youths were paranoia-addled by the plant, their minds a ticker tape of images alarming, and voices they'd effaced slipped their fetters and rampaged through their consciousness. *Ska* was slowed to speeds of torpor, and dancers spun and swerved like those who spoke the songs of birds, for their bodies had surrendered. If this was the direction *ska* was going—sluggish; droopy—Jane was worried. Some played instruments of *ska* and also soccer at the very same time, a practice Morgan witnessed on the streets, but still could not accept, as if his eyes were liars.

Then there were widows who knelt beside grief-shrines and wept. I hate it here, said Jane. We look pathetic. All we do is get fucked up or make stupid noises. No one is in charge. We're the shit of the earth; we're history's victims. Morgan didn't want to say it, but he'd always been relieved to be a Swede, for Gypsies seemed wretched.

The tiny cigarette had made its way to Billy, who whirled a clumsy pirouette and bashed some fellow spinners, with all the nearby Gypsies shocked at his inelegance. We have to get out of here, said Jane, who looked away from Morgan in a motion of tearfulness concealed, which he, who cried so often, recognized. He had never seen her sad before, and took her arm. Watch this.

He summoned cavern-doves and pigeons, crows and kites and ravens, and every one-eyed, wingless broken bird that he could find, and drew them all together, slowly, in a funnel-shape, until a squirming bird tornado writhed above their heads. Gypsies momentarily were rapt, but turned to look at Morgan, who they had always feared for his ambivalence to them, and resented, for his power over birds, though in their secret private hearts, they loved his dangerous fearless reputation, who had never once surrendered, no matter how much RedBlacks beat him. Gypsies wished he was a Gypsy, so he could be their leader, but kept their desperation secret, and looked at him with caution.

Morgan gestured at his heart in what he hoped would be received as a signal of his oneness with the Gypsies. They were puzzled, and a thousand Gypsies shrugged. I'm one of you, he said. He's one of us, they said, adjusting to the news. He's one of us. The Bird Boy is one of us.

Gypsies screamed in joy, in absolute abandon. They cried his name in rapture, danced and sang in ecstasy, calling him a prophet, a messiah. The tornado spun faster. It was here, at this moment, that the boy became a star; the Gypsies started mobbing all his birdshows, and showed their fealty to him, their absolute devotion to the one they called the Bird Boy, a symbol from above that they would never be abandoned by their god, or so they tried to think. Their loyalty to him was unconditional, from that instant in the tunnels, with his pigeon-dove tornado.

We aren't weak, he said to Jane. We're the kings of the city.

Billy joined the celebration in the Megachurch, while Jane and Morgan kissed. She wasn't really sure what Morgan had accomplished, but he trafficked in these massive demonstrations, which seemed to carry everyone away, past the barriers of awe, to new kinds of belief, a Morgancentric hagiography. She felt skeptical of anyone who worshipped him, and yet he was her boyfriend.

Back in her apartment, he thrust himself against her, and no sooner had she prized him from his pants than he expended, with a gasp, on her leg, which she had bared by pulling up her skirt, her manner more or less as fumbling as his. He drew closer every day to his goal of sexual intercourse, and Jane made known that she was pleased her first encounter with "the act" would take place in the arms of an expert.

Morgan shuddered. He hadn't been especially forthcoming with the truth of his "experience," furnishing instead a bunch of lies. He panicked. She would know he'd been dishonest; he would be terrible in bed, and she would tease him, or snitch to all his fans, and, god forbid, to Billy. He pretended to be sick and ran home.

He avoided Jane for days and wouldn't meet her underground. The world was poisoned with his lie of sexual prowess, the disgrace that he would feel when she exposed him had afflicted him already. How could he have been so dumb as to be snared within a trap of his own making? He had never been so miserable; the courage he had showed when RedBlacks caught him in the tunnels offered him no solace, spoke no wisdom. Had he really been courageous, ever? He didn't know; his sexual failure seemed to vaporize his history. Everything was silent in the face of this unhappiness. Zvominir asked was he okay, and he was too afraid to answer. He felt surprised the birds still obeyed him.

He told himself he'd never cared for Jane, it had all been some mistake, he would make himself forget her. He would gain his sexual expertise from someone else, perhaps from a professional. He kept on boasting to his RedBlacks of his conquests, and they shook their heads resentfully, muttering how easy it would be to score if they had his power. Birdshows were so popular that Morgan could console himself with looks of admiration from girls he didn't know, and wouldn't have to disappoint. Still, Billy took his spot among the audience, his look of friendship undiminished. Morgan wrongly assumed Billy knew what had happened between him and Jane. He missed how he and Billy'd banged around the streets and in the tunnels, partying and listening to *ska*. He'd enjoyed having someone who esteemed him, and felt too scared to steal on his own, while Billy had no fear. Plus, Billy loved getting drunk, and knew where all the *ska* bands played. Morgan couldn't find them on his own.

But he finally bumped into Jane near his apartment, on his way home from his job. He said it wasn't a good time, he was tired and surrounded by his RedBlacks, who he wanted to impress. When Jane suggested they go inside to his room, he tried to put her off. Lovers' quarrel, said the RedBlacks, and Jane was livid for how Morgan wouldn't take her side before the soldiers.

They went into his little room, and sat down on his mattress; beneath it was the hole into the tunnels Morgan hadn't used in days, which had been covered up by tiles until Jane found it. Her lovely face had gone despondent, and she could hardly meet his gaze without tears. She was vulnerable to pain, which surprised him; he had made himself believe that she was merciless, but Jane had not been merciless with him, she had only been sweet. He had betrayed her. Why are you avoiding me, she asked. What did I do? She clearly blamed herself, and Morgan acted cold, to perpetuate the notion that their split had been her fault.

She said she had deduced he was a virgin, she had all along suspected it. He strove to discredit this assumption, and rued that he lied badly, but he also found her generous, compassionate demeanor too strong to resist. Jane was attractive, and he needed forgiveness, for she'd revealed an insincerity in him, exposed him to himself in a way he didn't like, and would do anything to stop. He had sworn to have the power over her, but in the end, it was she who agreed to take him back, and he who begged.

They finally fucked, a bond the more emotional for the awkward way they forged it. Later, they found Billy in the tunnels, and stole a bottle of champagne from a liquor store. He saw that he had friends, he had a girlfriend, and the family he hadn't known he wanted.

15

Morgan used the hole in the floor of his bedroom to slip into the tunnels, where he paired off with Jane, while Billy went off on his own.

Billy looked across an empty street at a group of rich and pretty girls named Carrie, Jesse, Kara and Jody. They clustered and laughed, heedless of Billy, their moist and shiny perfect skin reflecting light. The girls he knew didn't look that clean, and didn't own clothes like that. They stood beneath a string of lamps that dangled from an arch that linked together two opposing buildings. He found himself wanting to kiss behind their knees, and what an odd impulse that was; he really should just want to rob them, to yell at them for growing up so rich and happy-looking, so giddy and oblivious with privilege. But in his heart, he was not a robber. Despite all his experience and skill, he had never been the person Jane expected him to be; he just wanted to have fun. Having Morgan around just made the contradiction worse. He felt had to prove himself to both of them.

For sure he wouldn't rob the girls, he wanted them to love him, or at least to like him, certainly to sleep with him. He wanted them against his better judgment. Morgan and Jane would've criticized him thus, they always told him what to do.

He'd gone back to stores they'd burglarized and left apologetic notes.

The girls had left the arch, and he tailed them through the streets, between the outdoor café tables lit by bluegreen candles. Watching them laugh, he felt friendless, and ashamed to be alone. Now would be the moment to pounce against the girls, who passed the tiny cigarette—he could sell them drugs!—laughing more and wobbling a bit on pointy shoes unsuited to the cobblestones. Billy wore his only pair of shoes: boots with holes. He'd stolen many shoes with Jane and Morgan, but didn't wear them, and gave them out to anyone who asked, or sold them in the tunnels, always at a lower price than Jane and Morgan fetched. Billy haggled badly, and pitied those he haggled with. The point of haggling seemed to be to cheat folks out of money, and Billy hated cheating. Buy low, Morgan told him, and sell high. That's what the Judge does. You should see his house.

You said you didn't want a house, Billy said. You want revenge, for your swans. I do want revenge, and to get it, I need power, and power comes with money, so I need money. Morgan is sometimes full of shit, Billy thought, yet Billy kept on wanting to impress him, for Morgan wasn't scared to fight. He had courage.

Billy tailed the girls to an outdoor bar, where a group of off-duty RedBlacks called them to their table. The soldiers, with their plastic-looking hair

and bulging muscles honed, no doubt, on practice fields enjoyed in expensive distant legend-
ary schools, seemed experts in the crucial art of
flirting. Everything they said got laughs, it was
incredible; they seemed so free of doubt. His own
face was a puzzle of uncertainty. Billy sat alone at
a table and watched as RedBlacks rallied around
their looks and flair. He felt jealous.

A waiter dressed in sailor's clothes came to
his table. The bar, Billy saw, had a nautical theme,
the tables were fenced by what looked like the
rails of a ship, and a boat-shaped billboard overhead cried *Anchors Away!* Billy ordered orange
juice. He liked orange juice. One could rarely find
a decent orange, even in the tunnels. The waiter
advised him that the bar didn't serve orange juice,
and that, at any rate, his kind wasn't served there.
Oh, Billy said, I'm too young.

No, said the waiter. You're a Gypsy.

The waiter looked like a Gypsy, too, with his
pale skin, green eyes, red hair and beakish nose—
Gypsies, Morgan had said, all look the same.
You're a Gypsy, too, said Billy. I told you to leave,
said the waiter. You're a traitor, Billy said. Look,
man, I'm trying to make a living, don't screw it
up for me. Is money all you care about? So what
if it is?

Billy stood and left, enraged, but still afraid
to fight. The girls hadn't noticed the affair with the
waiter, they had boys to pay attention to. Billy hid

behind a tree and continued spying on their table, where nobody seemed short of words or indecisive, socially. How do they know what to say, Billy wondered; he hardly spoke jovially with anyone. Mostly, Jane and Morgan teased him. He could hear their voices tell him to not be a pussy.

The girls had started pairing off with Red-Blacks; the soldiers slung their rifles over their shoulders, a gesture they enacted with a certain weary flair, as though the rifles were a burden, which they weren't. If you took away their rifles, Billy thought, who were they? This is your chance, Morgan would say; they don't have you outnumbered anymore. So pick the biggest RedBlack, follow him; attack him and prove yourself a hero.

Billy followed the prettiest girl. She clutched her massive RedBlack boyfriend's hand. Don't be afraid of his size, Morgan would've said, he won't expect you to attack him, they're all so conceited and they have so much to lose, that's how we're going to beat them. Jane would disapprove of all this stalking, by the way. She warned against direct confrontations, or any kind of fighting. Our goal, she said, is living off the grid. Violence is wrong. But Jane didn't quite understand how he felt: he looked up to Morgan. The RedBlack and his girl stopped to kiss, while Billy hid behind another tree. The girl and her RedBlack laughed again. Billy would've given anything to be that happy, he wished he could be both of them at once, but

he could not reveal this desire, and would have to
conceal it. He hoped, he prayed, to be the lie.

He stalked them to a bench beside a rose bush, finches in the trees sang their music. He pried up a cobblestone chunk with his shoe. His arms felt heavy, as if he dreamt he couldn't move. He wished he could wake up.

Now was not the time to be afraid.

He threw the rock as hard as he could, missed the guy and smacked the girl—*dok!*— in the tem- ple. She looked unshocked, almost annoyed, as if hit with a balled-up sock. Billy felt an ugly surge of failure. The girl fell off the bench, her RedBlack hadn't even seen the rock, and didn't know what had happened. But now, as he knelt beside her, he saw it on the ground, picked it up, put his ear to the girl's chest, and stood. He actually looked upset: the guy had feelings, and why not, the girl was dead. Billy wanted to apologize.

The soldier saw Billy, who turned to run. He shot him in the back.

16

The funeral procession for Billy crept along the streets of the ghetto as Gypsies crammed the route and blocked its progress, widows spurting tears and hurling flowers, men punching at the sky and cursing Billy's killer. A martyr, cried Jane, atop the coffin of her brother, and who were all the Gypsies to argue, most of them had never met her brother, they'd only come to this procession because they'd heard a rumor Morgan would be there. Everyone was furious and desperate, and the crowd effect but magnified their passions, as if, by putting mourning humans in immediate proximity to each other, you changed their grief to rage. Did Jane truly think that Billy was a martyr, or did she say it just to mollify her grief? Morgan wasn't sure what martyrs were. He stood beside her on the donkey-cart, while streams of solemn vultures flowed above them, parakeets and toucans at their feet. Jane hated toucans, she announced, for their stupid, over-colored beaks; Get these fucking decorative birds out of my sight.

Billy had been dead for seven days. Jane had been afraid the RedBlacks would arrest her if she came to claim the body, and the corpse had finally been discharged when there seemed to be no next of kin. She was disconsolate every day before the funeral; by the time of the parade, she'd oversuffered.

Morgan suffered too, for Billy was his friend, and Jane his lover, so her misery was his, to some extent, but the Bird Man complicated Morgan's grief, as Billy'd killed a girl himself. It's certainly unfortunate, said Zvominir, but don't get dumb about it. Your friend had it coming. Zvominir himself had de-birded at the dead girl's funeral, where many people also cried, such as her parents. Morgan screamed at Zvominir for saying this, but he could have no simple sorrow now.

Billy was a martyr, Jane repeated, an example all Gypsies should follow. Morgan, nodded yes, Billy was a martyr, though he wasn't sure why anyone should want to follow the example Billy set and get killed for no reason. Nonetheless, he waved at kids he recognized from birdshows, and told them *Billy was a martyr*. The procession would march along the river of venus flytraps, to where the water actually flowed, and Billy would be tossed there.

The Gypsies howled and banged on drums, and aimed their grimaces above, at vulture-clouds. Look at all this wasted energy, said Jane. If we could only harness it.

They tossed Billy's body on a pyre that someone lit, but Jane did not participate, the brother she had known was dead. She said she wasn't sentimental, only angry. A couple venus flytraps winked obscenely at the mourners. Jane wasn't looking at the flytraps, she scowled back at the city with an anger-face that Morgan didn't like. He stood alone by the riverbank as birds flew in circles overhead, slow and regal, in memory of Billy, plus he had to keep the vultures busy so they wouldn't eat his dead friend, and the Gypsies stopped to watch and wept again. Morgan made the vultures imitate the rolling of the waves, with pigeons for the flashing of sun; a cardinal flew in place below the flow of birds, representing Billy. The Gypsies started chanting Morgan's name. Jane asked what was he was doing, and he said, Honoring Billy, but she said, Entertainment isn't honor. Honor him with deeds.

She wouldn't talk the whole way back.

When he met her in the tunnels later on, she made him wear a balaclava and a hood. She seized him by the throat and swore she was no mourner of the tunnels, she would have revenge. They broke into a library, and spent hours stealing armfuls of schematics, blueprints, maps, and urban planning documents. Jane kept telling him to hurry as he gasped up and down the many steps, and ran through endless rows of books. Way to get revenge, he said. Read some books. What did you do for your swans, she asked. Get a job with their murderers? You're a coward and a phony, and worse than your father, at least he doesn't lie about it.

He'd only wanted to be funny. What the hell is wrong with you, he asked. I hate bullshit now, she said. And we're going to overthrow the city, in Billy's name.

He helped her hide the stolen objects in the tunnels, under manholes, deep in cracks he'd never seen, and behind so many different false walls that even under torture he could never say where they all were.

The next night, things were different.

17

She called it Night One Of The Rebellion.

From here on out, her face would be concealed by the black balaclava and the hood. Keep your gloves on, she instructed, never leave a fingerprint, or touch a surface with your body, leave no trace except for ashes, we are fire. She'd flattened out the bottoms of shoes that were too big for his feet, and made him wear them, and also made him wear a belt of weights; RedBlacks would calculate his mass from the size, tread and depth of his shoe-prints. She wore weights as well, and shoes for boys, and they would never know she was a girl, they would die chasing boys until she'd finished off them all, in Billy's name, their martyr.

She led him through the underground city, and seemed to go in circles, through passageways too thin for even him, in what seemed more like hazing than whatever rebel action she had planned, a test of his emotional endurance, which he passed because he acted like he didn't really care, though he did, and suppressed his truest doubts in the name of his allegiance to Jane, and in memory of Billy, though how can doubts be true if we don't act on them? She insisted they would never take the straight route again, would behave as if RedBlack agents tailed them, even underground. They were monks of anonymity. You're an asset to the cause in certain ways, she had said, but your identity will have to be contained while we're in action. Don't be so obsessed, he said. Jeez. RedBlacks, she said, when they see what we have done, will also be obsessed. We need to be perfectionists. What should Morgan say: Don't try so hard! Be worse at your job! Jane was right: he would draw too much attention.

After Morgan's demonstration in the Megachurch, the Gypsies had interpreted the power of the Bird Boy and his father as divine, and, because the boy had been brave in his defiance of the Red-Blacks, and positive toward Gypsies, they worshipped him. Clergy saw the need to not get left behind, and said that Morgan just might be a god, and while Jane commanded he ignore their advances, they praised him just the same, they were all drawn along, as by an undertow. The tunnels had transformed into a park of Bird Boy shrines, where people worshipped as he passed unsuspected, wearing weights beneath his shirt and floppy shoes appropriate for clowns, and sweating in his hood and balaclava. He didn't know how the shrine craze started; they all just seemingly appeared.

They came through a hole, and up into a bank, with barrel-vaulted ceilings, golden fixtures, rows of ivory counters, and shiny wooden overpolished desks, with chairs to match, where Morgan wanted to recline. Every surface gleamed to signify financial credibility, as if to say, if we can take care of these objects, we can care for your money. Morgan felt the thing he always felt in rooms like this, where voices echoed: he wanted to belong to a world that could generate this feeling, belong to beauty, give himself to beauty, if that was what this was. But Jane felt suspicious of beauty, which trafficked in desire, not in justice, and left you lonelier and sadder. It made you feel worse in the guise of feeling better, and left you hungry for more beauty. Further. It enfeebled you politically, by pointing at some hypothetical catharsis, a transcendence that could not be achieved, for who could really say they had communed with a non-religious paradise of aesthetics? The beauty effect: a crescendo of nothing. Beauty distracted from things that were important—the rights of disadvantaged people—in the name of something that it claimed was more important, and which didn't actually exist. It was a cognitive conspiracy, a con that disempowered. That's how Jane knew she would win: her people had no recourse to distraction, while the natives were obese from mental cake. She opened up her backpack, and handed Morgan jars of brown jelly. What are these, he asked.

Napalm, she said. He'd never heard of it.

Jane handed him a page with images and text

that instructed him on where to put the jars, which
she had drawn by hand, in a font he couldn't read,
for she had spent a day inventing characters that
no one could interpret. She was brilliant and annoying; her excellence could not abide the normal. He tried to put the jars where she had said,
to follow her directions and be faithful to the plan,
but she'd already gone off somewhere else, and he
was scared, and very bored, and her directions
were confusing, like huts or hieroglyphics. Plus,
he didn't like to read, and his hood and balaclava were uncomfortable. He took them off. When
she came back from wherever she had gone, the
backpack she had used to haul the jars was full
of money. She also carried sacks of bills, one of
which she gave to Morgan, and declared it their
nest egg. Banks would finance her endeavor, they
would buy their own demise, and she stole money now before the RedBlacks thought to mark it.
Time to buy a dress, Morgan said. Put your mask
and hood back on, she said. She refused to even
laugh anymore. You do the napalm like I said?

Yes. She checked his work, like some pedan-
tic evil schoolteacher Morgan never had. What
a fucking mess, said Jane, and looked at her
watch. He found this new routine distasteful. She
marched to where he stood behind a row of teller
windows, and pointed to the map, which he still
held in his hand. This pattern, she said, which
you can't seem to make with jars, forms a capi-

tal "G." It stands for Gypsy. Get it? Dickhead. A quick look at the map proved she was right. He felt ashamed, and tried to make excuses, but why did everyone who really knew him—i.e. Zvominir and Jane—seem to hate him? Jane laid the wick along the G of jars, and ran it back to the hole. The wick smelled of fuel; she had made it herself, like the napalm. She tossed a Molotov Cocktail in the vaults, to burn the money she had soaked with napalm, and, when she and Morgan climbed into the tunnel, she lit the string. They paused at the bottom of the hole to smell the smoke, and hear the fire's sound, like a stampede overhead.

She hid the money in a tunnel hole concealed behind a bird-shrine, and stuffed the hole with carcasses of rats she'd doctored to appear freshly dead, to throw off any busybodies. Also in this hole were two more backpacks, and the kind of yellow bucket one associates with mops, though its castors had been glued in one direction, to ensure it rolled true. She took the backpacks, handed one to Morgan, and made him take the bucket. When he didn't move as quickly as she liked, she led him by the hand, which she clenched until he thought his knuckles would be ground up into gravel. She wouldn't say where they were headed. It would scare him if he knew.

Her destination was a crevice, a crack in the foundation of a building. She checked her watch and checked her watch and nearly wore it out with looking, and scrambled up the fissure, with Morgan behind her. This hole's too narrow for a spider, he said. They could hardly pass the backpack and the bucket through this cleft, let alone their bodies, yet they climbed seven feet above the tunnel floor, and she ordered him to brace himself, and not to make a sound. From his perch in the crevasse, he watched her place a backpack full of napalm in the bucket. He also saw light, which seemed to signify a slightly opened door. In the brightness, he could see more buckets, brooms, mops, and also bottles, such as those which hold ammonia, or other cleaning products. Perhaps it was the closet of a janitor.

Morgan smelled a burning, and the creaky sound of rolling little wheels found his ears. Jane closed the door and ordered Morgan to make haste underground, and used obscenities to motivate him, her manner so profane he stayed in place to piss her off. He fumed that she would speak to him this way, and felt angry for the whole bloody night, though, also, it was hard to move in his position, for he was like an object caught between teeth. Jane kicked his head.

Morgan heard the backpack explode, and Jane was crying, Hurry! Fuck! Fuck! A second, giant, blast shook her loose, and sent her tumbling down upon him, along with chunks of the crevasse, which very soon had all but closed, for more immense explosions followed, eruptions so severe the tunnel shook enough to keep them off their feet. They had landed in a heap, and yet, in the chaos, Jane checked her watch and said, Come on. Behind them, fire drooled through the cracks in the tunnel. The eruptions struck like drumrolls for their speed, and earthquakes for their power.

They blew up one more building: a storefront that sold donuts, and was popular with RedBlacks. The seizures of the Earth ceased at last. Beyond the river, past the hills of Oklahoma, the sun had started rising, like a fire in the sky unleashed by Jane, in Billy's name, a martyr. RedBlacks scrambled through the smoky light of dawn, they were unprepared and frantic, for war had found them decadent and ready to be vanquished, inadequate to Jane, who watched from a rooftop.

We awoke to horror and perplexity. The arson at the bank had engaged the RedBlacks of a precinct house that also happened to include an ammunition dump. Jane drew the soldiers to the bank, then attacked their armory: rolled a bucket full of napalm to the storage room door and blew it in, gambling she'd ignite at least one bullet with her flaming gobs of glop, and start a chain reaction. It had worked: a three-block radius had simply disappeared, as though God himself had stepped on it. Finally, she'd destroyed the local donut shop, just to add a final insult. A hundred RedBlacks stood beside the ruin of their old hangout and cursed their new and ruthless foe.

Jane checked her watch, and beamed from within her balaclava. Three buildings in seventy-one minutes, she said. We can beat the RedBlacks. Morgan knew he should he happy, he had wanted to destroy things, or thought he had, but now he didn't know what to want. He was terrified. He was close to throwing up.

Billy would be proud of us, she said. Billy thought you were a pacifist, Morgan said.

I used to believe in pacifism. Now I believe in this.

18

Zvominir watched Mrs. Giggs kneel beside a bed of philodendrons, cradling the petals and frowning. She appeared to be killing the flowers—the Swede could not believe his eyes—pulling up the healthy ones and placing them neatly in her satchel, working from flowerbed to flowerbed, methodically and slowly, and though she had a long way to go before the gardens were destroyed, she seemed devoted to the process. Gardeners, meanwhile, toiled in different regions of the yard, and found the vandalized flowers. Mrs. Giggs wrote their schedule. You go this way, she would say, and I go that way.

Zvominir went upstairs to a balcony, the best place to de-bird. Katherine met him there, as always, and looked her usual miserable. They watched Mrs. Giggs examine flowers, inspecting every single petal, a pedant of decay. She picked her way through flower glitters that cascaded down the wide and sloping yard. Zvominir held a million or so mergansers in place above the house, stalling before he sent them off, as Katherine liked the ritual.

The soldiers were still under orders to bring Katherine home straight after school. The girl had tried to leave her house, but RedBlacks met her at the gates, and ordered her inside. Days went

by and she went nowhere but school. Her mother
never left the house either; they were solitude's
twins. Even when Katherine walked the paths of
the garden, soldiers watched her, loitering at corners or spying from treetops, and more at home
in the mansion than she was. They dwelled at the
gates and in the kitchen, where they ate, played
poker on the driveway, and napped outside the
stables. There was no place she could go except
her bedroom and feel comfortable.

19

Elsewhere in the yard, beside a row of rutabagas, someone studied Katherine as she stood on the balcony, or what little could be seen of her, though, even from a distance, she was perfect. This was the tutor, a young and gifted soldier whom the Judge had hired after the bazooka episode to teach Mike how to act. He leaned on an old, wood fence beside a pond where mallards trashed the water with their flapping. The voices of the ducks had a low, brooding quality, as if they mourned loves impossible.

Staring at my sister again, asked Mike, who had walked up unseen.

Of course not, said the tutor, I have no idea what you're talking about. Shouldn't you be with your father?

Mike said his father had thrown him out of his office. There had been a meeting about the "Gypsy Challenge"—Why had they come here? How could we make them leave? Mass torture? It was surely worth a shot!—but Mike had been tossed for drunken blurting. The tutor wondered what impertinent thing Mike could have said. The failures of the rich and overprivileged had always pleased the tutor, but now he was responsible for the city's most unpromising debutard. What did I teach you about getting drunk in public, asked the tutor. I really couldn't tell you, Mike said, I wasn't listening. You want to play some cards? He tromped down the footpath to a grove of sequoias, where his friends, the RedBlack duo who had beaten up the Swedes, loudly snored, like bears in caves. Their names were Tom and Gus. We would individuate them further, but we can't; a paucity of evidence prevents us. We imagine them handsome and mean, and one was taller than the other.

Mike kicked the two rather harder than was called for, and handed them a flask. Your father might sniff your breath, said the tutor. Blow me, said Mike. They got us on garden detail, Tom said, we pull up weeds all day. When do we get privileges for being your friends?

The tutor tried explaining that the gardens were the city's precious legacy, but Mike and Tom and Gus all said, Shut up. Gus dealt the cards. The tutor had been first in his RedBlack class, but didn't like to fight at all—he hated causing pain in other humans, and causing pain was a RedBlack's raison d'etre, modus operendi, and every other foreign word—yet his grades and manners were impeccable. The Judge learned about the tutor when the Swedes had escaped into the tunnels. The tutor made the plan which resulted in their capture, he'd known exactly where the Bird Man and his son would be hiding. He knew where to send the troops, and how to get them orders underground;

he had spied on the Swedes in the Square, in the first days of the bird-invasion. He also thanked superior officers, and didn't get drunk, like Mike did. He had studied all of the maneuvers made by Hungary, China and Algeria throughout our wars of glory. The kid was impressive, and yet, despite his many gifts, his superiors insisted he was simply scared to fight, he froze during drills, and couldn't point a gun at something living. Hard to get it all in one package, thought the Judge. Nonetheless, he's perfect for my purposes.

The Judge and tutor had a confab, in the Giggs house office, where towering walls of cloudy white intermingled with old, squat walls of wood paneling. The tutor felt bewildered, for this office, and, indeed, the whole building, made no sense. He thought he heard his thoughts here, his fears and regrets, but not within his mind; they seemed to echo in the walls, somehow. It was impossible to explain, and seemed intentional, and it scared him.

You don't really want be a soldier, said the Judge. No, the tutor said, my parents are poor, and a career in the RedBlacks was the only way I had of making money. The Judge nodded. I suppose that you don't want to read my poems, said the boy. Do I look like a fag, asked the Judge.

The Judge clapped the boy on the shoulder and said, Listen, son, you're never going to make it in the military, you're too much of a pussy. You would, however, make a splendid teacher, and I have the perfect student: my own son Mike, such as he is. The tutor tried to not react, so frightened did he feel of showing that he knew of Mike's problems, his drunkenness and penchant for rudeness, mangled syntax and calamitous mistakes, like the scene with the bazooka. Go ahead, said the Judge, say you've never heard of Mike. Say you don't know about his ignorance and cruelty. No sir, I don't, nor would I be at liberty to repeat such things if in fact I did know them, they would die in me, I would be their silent graveyard. You're a crappy liar, said the Judge, I see how you fold up in a fight.

The Judge may be perceptive, thought the tutor, but what the old guy didn't know was that the tunnel-search plan for the Swedes had succeeded based on little more than luck. The sewers into which the Swedes had fled were the only set of tunnels in the city that were mapped. If Zvominir and Morgan had wandered even one block further in any direction, they would never have been caught. At least you see the need to lie strategically, said the Judge. Mike doesn't. You're hired. Turn my son into you, except don't make him a coward, just make him smart. My wife expects me to fail, she thinks I'll ram my kids into their graves. You're going to help me prove her wrong.

Now the tutor sat with Mike, Tom and Gus, and watched them playing cards. Seeing Mike lose, he whispered instructions, which made Tom and Gus object, especially since Mike had started winning. The tutor knew strategy; you should've seen him play chess.

He's teaching me, said Mike, pocketing the money. If you're so smart, said Gus, why do you like Mike's sister?

The tutor turned almost purple.

If you're so smart, Mike said, you'd figure out a way to kill the Bird Boy. You'd get his sister then, Tom said. That's who she likes. Mike punched Tom in the chest and said, Don't ever say my sister likes a Gypsy.

The sound of Gypsy music whooped up close all of a sudden. The band had arrived, and boomed out their *ska*, while simultaneously running. Mike grinned, and tore off through the yard, with Tom and Gus in pursuit, while the tutor stayed behind. Mike liked to have his Gypsies chase him as they played, through the gardens and the streets of the city. Some kind of chasing fetish, thought the tutor, who tried and failed to keep the pace. He didn't like to run. It puzzled him that Gypsies who were fat, old, chainsmokers with bad shoes could both play their instruments and run at the same exact time. Mike should give the lessons on living, not him.

The clarinetist Chico taught Mike to play. Learning an instrument was thought to broaden the horizons, so to speak, and Mike could surely profit from a full-scale enlargement of his mind. On the other hand, the band spent all day playing music, getting smashed and smoking cigarettes they'd rolled themselves, with questionable tobacco. Could such indulgence really aid the studies of a person who didn't need to learn to party, but to concentrate?

Mike loved to run with Chico, and Chico must've liked Mike. The boy excelled at running, but his clarinet technique was grotesque, his pitch and ear for sound so bad they made the birds cry out in pain. Still, Chico timed his sprints with a stopwatch, and the promoter kept a record of his progress, so Mike, competitive as he was, never thought of quitting. The tutor knew his lectures were inferior to this loony pursuit.

The tutor looked up toward the balcony again. It was empty. Katherine had gone.

20 Katherine: earnest, mousy, with an urge to be greater than she was. A painfully serious and adorable young woman, if not quite a pretty one. The tutor thought he was superior to her: smarter, more ambitious, and certain to succeed on his own merits, but Katherine had rejected his advances. In retrospect, he'd been arrogant and clumsy; he'd boasted of his genius in their first conversation. The second time they spoke, he wrote a poem for her. He'd heard she liked poems. He said he'd cook a giant dinner. He was fabulous with garlic! She continued to reject him. Her academic standing was reputable, and he said he could make connections in that world, maybe get her into college. Still, rejection. This humiliated the tutor, who, at first, had only had an interest in the girl out of pity. He realized that the promise of connections meant nothing to the daughter of the city's most connected man. She wasn't all that cute—or rather, she was no more than cute, though cute, while often a cliché, could hurt you more than beauty, for beauty is forthrightly, hopelessly remote and strange to the mind, while cuteness seems available, as Katherine seemed available, and yes, as a beauty, she was flawed, but her cuteness was extreme—but now he was obsessed. He knew she might not be remarkable at all; she might be nothing. But desire inflamed the eye.

He wouldn't tell Katherine of the other job the Judge had given him besides teaching Mike: finding the Gypsy who had bombed three buildings in the city. The tutor had already drawn some formulas, and the first thing he had found was the attacks—and those that followed, there were many, and seemed the work of the same Gypsy—were unnervingly meticulous. The fires said something, which he couldn't yet interpret, and his hunch—that the arsons weren't an impulse, weren't sexual, as such, but were a movement—were too bleak to be spoken without proof. RedBlacks never felt endangered by the Gypsies, for Gypsies had always been stupid. What if they weren't stupid anymore? What if—gads!—they'd evolved?

The tutor left Mike and looked for Katherine, trying to provoke a lucky bumping-into and listening for echoes and little sound-reflections, the Giggs house seemed to hoard so many voices. He drew a little sound-map on the back page of Mike's syllabus. The echoes had no systematic pattern he could find; voices seemed to reappear in places nowhere near where they'd been spoken. He had caught drifts of the voice of the Judge from an area near the front door, had stood there and eavesdropped as Mike romped with his band; the Judge discussing murder and parrots. Within the liquor closet and its watered-down Scotch, or, as Mike said Katherine called it, *Scottish*, he could hear the Judge's office, had heard the Judge screaming at his wife, and her silent riposte. *You don't talk to the kids anymore, and you don't talk to me, you think Mike will fail; you think Katherine's going down the wrong path, you blame me for Charlie, and you think the same will happen to them; you think I'm going to fail, you think they'll die like Charlie, you're practically rooting for it; someone's ruining the gardens, did you know that? Is it you?*

All of this is going to be destroyed, she said. *We'll be responsible again. I can't stand it.*

You think the birds are here because of me, of what I've done, he said, *but they are just a challenge, I will meet like I've met the others. This is not my ending, do you hear, it is not, it is not, it is not.*

The second-floor balconies eavesdropped on the kitchen; he could hear the garden from the stairs until the shrubs were trimmed; the sound disappeared and popped up near the Judge's bedroom. The tutor ducked in doorways, hid from passing soldiers, shuffled through his notes, looking busy, blending in, keeping watch for Katherine, a rare sight even in her home, so often in her room or with the Swede on his bird-rounds.

His theory: the Giggs house wandered like a mind, like a consciousness in torment. As such, he couldn't really know it, and only knew he didn't know it. You may ask why he failed to understand the echoes, while Katherine succeeded. The answer is the house was of her family.

He made his way to the third-floor balcony, where Katherine had been, but from the landing, he saw her in the garden with the Swede, smiling and talking as he broke up the bird-flocks and sent them away. Katherine talked incessantly to Zvominir, she practically babbled. Lucky Swede, who filled his ears with Katherine! She hardly said a word to the tutor. She seemed more comfortable with servants than peers, and with anybody but her mother.

The tutor knew he shouldn't get involved in Katherine's life. He shouldn't probe the shadows of the Giggs house in search of her, or monitor gossip that concerned her, or keep a set of maps of sounds she'd made inside her house. He should've ignored her from the start. But he couldn't. He could not control his mind. The tutor thought of Katherine in his military dorm, the small room he shared with three other RedBlacks who drank and played cards until dawn, keeping him awake to think of Katherine; he thought of her while eating alone in the mess hall as she ate alone in her kitchen, her silent mother brooding the garden or in bed, the Judge signing warrants in his office, her brother passed out, having just stumbled home, his band in a heap on the lawn. She would ride to school in a carriage ringed by RedBlacks, her face concealed behind a metal door, the school under guard and protected; the tutor passed by on his horse. The tutor wished he could be Katherine's teacher. He wanted to grade her essays, watch her fiddle with her hair, call her in for conferences, pry her open like—and here he struggled for an image that would not be a cliché—a hidden chest of treasure.

Alas, he was smart, but not the poet he wished he was.

He thought of her the whole time he tried teaching Mike, who wouldn't pay attention and brought his band and friends everywhere, who failed the assignments from his father and couldn't discern simple hints. At lunch, the tutor ate alone among the peonies, traced the paths that Katherine walked, the trails among the trellises of lilac and wisteria that sent her voice into the house to mingle with the parrot-blurts, her mother and the Judge. He knew Katherine ate her lunch alone, he'd checked reports; Mike ate with his friends, and thundered through the gardens with his band. The tutor liked to think of Katherine listening to the lectures that drove Mike into stupors. He had seen her squirm at state engagements, trapped in formal clothes, like a cat in a dress. It made him want her more. In the meantime, he made do with paid women, though he felt they overcharged him. At night, his bunkmates teased him too much for him to sleep, not that he would've slept anyway.

21

The tutor watched from the third-floor balcony as Katherine and the Swede roamed the flowers, and engaged single birds. The Judge arrived, slipped into the scene without so much as crushing leaves beneath his feet, or making any noise at all, as silent as the reaper. Katherine, he said, and kissed her cheek, I need some time alone with my Gypsy. Katherine said, he's a Swede. Why, I know, my little know-itall, I'm teasing. Maybe tonight we can go into the city, walk the streets and get some ice cream. Katherine smiled and ran off for the house.

The Judge and his daughter were an interesting pair, thought the tutor. They acted like best friends. For the Judge, she was a kind of funhouse mirror which made him seem better than he was, and not responsible for certain things in history, such as suffering, torture, wars, and Charlie. He liked to hear himself sound delightful; he was the perfect audience for his own performance, and his daughter was a kind of trans-narcissistic object. The Judge was often over-friendly, and solicitously charming. It was his contradiction. Every person in the city knew that his charm was scary, except for Katherine.

Katherine loved the Judge because he was her father, and he had only ever been sweet, though his tenderness was founded on self-inter-est, and hers on insufficient information. Some-day, thought the tutor, she would learn what he actually had done, but she'd be too beholden to him then, too much of a Giggs, to be cleansed of his sin.

The Judge turned to the Swede.

I apologize ahead of time, said Zvominir, Whatever it was, I didn't mean it.

Why are there still parrots in my house?

I can't get them to leave, I take them away, but they come back.

Are you keeping them here to embarrass me? Are you fucking with me?

The Swede began to twitch. Your Honor, he said, I am just a man. I plead with the parrots, but they don't listen. I shall work harder and sweep the house twice a day. I swear I will do better.

He ran inside to find the birds. The Judge looked up at the balcony, pointed at the tutor and called out, Stay there. Then he made his way up the stairs, which took about eight minutes, such were the distances traversed. The tutor imagined all the ways he might be tortured, ways he knew from the official torture handbook, which the RedBlacks said did not exist, and this hurt him to hear, for he had been its editor, though he himself had never tortured anyone. He considered it bar-baric. But the manual he wrote was praised by all the officers, and the soldiers liked to use it, and the tutor simply loved to be admired. His need to be extolled outweighed his conscience.

The Judge walked on the balcony and stood beside the tutor, made him press against the balcony's black metal grate.

You are failing me, he said.

The tutor was trembling.

Failing me and failing my son. He humiliates himself all the time. He is not making progress. The tutor had never been so scared. I will redouble my efforts, said the tutor. I don't give a crap about effort, said the Judge. Retriple your results. Or else.

22 Zvominir paced the café's little rooms, waiting up for Morgan. He checked his watch—twelve-thirty—stood outside, and asked the soldiers if they'd heard any news. They looked up from their card game, shook their heads, raised a bottle, offered him a swig. Booze would take the edge off, they assured him. Gunshots popped in the distance, small explosions and gunfire, a dialogue of bangbang. I pay you to know this, he said. You pay Noah, said the Red-Blacks. We don't see your money.

Zvominir returned to the kitchen. These balls won't suck themselves, cried the soldiers, and laughed until the Swede closed the door. He'd wanted to purchase the closet-sized apartment next door, knock down the separating wall, and make it his bedroom, but payoffs to Noah had drained him of cash. Moving to the suburbs wasn't possible; he could not afford his bribes, let alone a house. He lay down on his cot, stood up, shoved his hands into the pockets of his tattered pants and paced the apartment. Children played in the rat-dense alley behind the café, such an awful place for games. Zvominir hated cities. His wife had been the one who insisted that they come here, he'd preferred a farmhouse in the country, so many were abandoned. And yet, he had let her have her way. Now he was here and she was dead; maybe Morgan was as well. He'd only stayed because, as bad as things were here, with the poverty and violence and racism, etc, they were worse in other cities. He went outside another time and asked the soldiers what they'd heard. These nuts, they said.

At three forty-five in the morning, Morgan came through the front door, streaked with soot, the new shirt Zvominir had bought him greased and ruined. Zvominir had worked in the suburbs all day, and he'd forgotten that a child could look so awful. Where have you been, he asked, but Morgan didn't answer, he stormed into his room and slammed the door. I burned a row of buildings, Morgan said. They all belonged to RedBlack motherfuckers. You'll hear about it tomorrow.

He begged his son to stop, and ordered him, and said they would be killed. The city needs us, he said, it's such a great opportunity, so can't you find a way to feel a part of things? The city needs to be re-organized, said Morgan, it isn't fair here, people suffer all the time, and yet you kiss the Judge's ass. Zvominir banged the door, and traded rants with his son.

The Swede confronted Noah in the morning. You're supposed to be protecting him, he said, but you keep letting him escape.

Noah wouldn't meet his gaze. The price went up, he said. Didn't you get the memo? What memo? Noah said the rate had tripled. He couldn't look the Bird Man in the face. I don't have that kind of money, no one does. Noah shrugged and said, No money, no watchee.

This isn't fair, Zvominir said, as much to the gods as to Noah. His raise had left him poorer than he'd been. I'm not his father, Noah said, Why don't you raise him better, instead of letting him turn into a juvenile delinquent? The RedBlacks all smiled and nodded, and passed around another bottle. What if he gets killed, said the Swede. Then he gets killed, Noah said, and we can finally go home.

Gunshots echoed in the neighborhood. People screamed in the distance. Something seemed to have galvanized the Gypsies into action. Zvominir prayed that Morgan wasn't part of it.

23

Morgan and his father may have had the power over birds, but Jane had a vision. The Judge, she said, could lose a war to insurgents who were mobile and strategically disorganized. The key would be the fact that RedBlacks had no way to navigate the tunnels, no floorplans or maps. The underground city was built to fight Hungarians, independent cells had carved it without specific knowledge of what the other groups were doing. They also fought as cells, which made them too nimble to directly engage. This had been the Judge's brilliant gift to warcraft, his magnificent idea, and would also be his downfall, for now he had a big and clumsy bureaucratic army, so hierarchical they had to fill out twenty forms just to march across the street. The Gypsies could freely cavort underground, attack and retreat, regroup and re-supply at will. All we have to do, she said, is re-conceive our desperate conditions as a kind of opportunity, our desperation as a freedom from encumbrance. RedBlacks will be busy typing paperwork, Jane said, and we'll be winning.

The Judge, she continued telling Morgan, had been too insecure at the end of the war, too paranoid and crazed for authority, so he unified the city by offering to welcome back the leaders

155

of the various militias he had deputized, and give them jobs in his regime. Those who came back to the fold he swiftly purged, and hunted to extinction those who didn't. The city had a large upper-middle class who valued stable government, which helped the Judge, who cloyed them with the promise of normalcy. But he and his Red-Blacks could be thwarted by the same kinds of tactics they themselves had used.

She had found banned public documents on sale in the tunnels, and ordered military history books from other countries. She'd tried to lure the RedBlacks underground, and they never, ever followed, except at one location, which they'd used the day they found the Swedes, after Mike's bazooka episode. She robbed a bank and paid some Gypsies to seal this entrance sealed from below, and helped to do the work herself. She liked to sweat.

Thus did Jane and Morgan start their fires every night, come up from the tunnels into stores, banks, offices and restaurants in wealthy neighborhoods, plant the brown jars in a glyph of Jane's selection, light the flames, and scramble underground. The tunnels were a city of their own, and every building had a hole, a closet or a crawl space, a door beneath the stairs; no building was an island. Your home has one, too.

Unlike her predecessor Gypsy rebel bombers, Jane had a system to determine where her fires would be set. She stole law enforcement theory books, and taught herself the formulae cops used to game criminals. She plotted snowflake patterns on the map, and thought up sneaky ways of adding accidental elements, so she could not be predicted. She called her plan *Oulipo*. She selected an address, and asked three strangers in the tunnels to pick numbers, which she added or subtracted to the address of the building she had chosen. Because she could suppress herself from the equation, she could generate a truly random target. She had set a hundred fires, and watched from rooftops as RedBlacks scurried hopelessly around with no chance in hell of catching her. They either sent too many soldiers, or too few, and they were always late; their failures at establishing security left them paralyzed with dread. They—we—were helpless, and we knew it. She would do to us what Hungary had done, but with stealth; this terror stuff is easy, she mused. Who needs armies? She was poor, and lived in sewers, so nothing could be taken but her life, while we had homes, jobs, children, hopes, dreams and possessions we adored, which all gave meaning to our lives. There was no end to that of which she could deprive us. Our privilege made us vulnerable.

It always warmed her heart, she said, to daydream of that room of thwarted male criminologists who'd been beaten by a girl, and not just any girl, but THE girl, Jane the Gypsy, who burned in the name of her murdered brother Billy, a martyr of the Gypsies.

Morgan's day began at six am, when Red-Blacks led by Noah picked him up. The Bird Boy would de-bird until mid-afternoon, and saw the many arson monuments to Jane, buildings he had helped to burn. The cinders crawled with scientists she'd conned by leaving chemicals behind as red herrings, whose first letters, taken together, spelled things like *God Hates You, Champ*. These men of science wept. Soon, the Judge sent priests. He was losing faith in reason. Morgan then returned to the Square for his birdshow, the best part of his life; people cheered him; girls squealed; his father disapproved, and so, increasingly, did Jane, who hated entertainment that distracted from her cause. Birdshows should galvanize, she said, and make converts of the audience. The birds should be seen as a fracture in reality, an army sent by god himself to hand the city to the Gypsies, and not as mere "amusement." Zvominir's perspective on the birds was the opposite: they should lead to peace for all, and security for the Swedes. Morgan's mind was like a battleground for Zvominir and Jane, and anything he thought was shouted down; he just liked the patterns he could make, and the cheers of the crowd.

Jane's critiques of his birdshows began to hurt him. She said she didn't think that he would ever be a leader, or even a figurehead. You're so insecure and vain, and you like applause too much, even from the families of RedBlacks, the very people you should demonize. They oppress you, and you kiss their ass. Your birdshows are so bloody unpolitical; they are all about you. But I'm an artist, Morgan said, you can't tell me what to make, I express my inner feelings. Artists can be critical, said Jane. What do you really stand for? Banging chicks? Approval from your enemies? I thought you wanted vengeance for your swans. You haven't mentioned them in weeks.

Mention of the swans piled misery on misery: he'd lost the battle in his head to blame their death on RedBlacks. He blamed himself. He hated Red-Blacks just as much as she did, but it was harder to be angry than before, it took effort, like a song he had sung too many times. Revenge had always seemed a daydream, soothing and improbable, and he didn't think he'd ever have to mean what he'd said. Plus, he was tired from his job. Now that he was busy all the time, he mostly acted mad to piss his father off. The goodwill he received from his birdshows couldn't help but make him happy, and who didn't want to be happy? Not that he didn't hate the Judge, but work took all the anger out of him. He didn't know what to think now, and leaders always had to know what they thought, their minds always seemed to calcify.

He didn't want to set her fires anymore, yet he felt he had a public duty to perform, of which she kept reminding him. Your job, Jane said, is to inspire us to courage, and make us hungry for our rights, not to preen for the audience. You have the gift, but not the mind that should attend it. She said it was unfair, and that she should have the gift, instead of him.

When the birdshow was over, he came home for a dinner with his father, which was frequently uncomfortable, and included many fights. Allegiance to the revolution seemed to mean he should reject this man, but Morgan had begun to feel nostalgic for the time before the plague of birds, when no one knew him and his dad, and there weren't any secrets or pressure. His father moved slowly, and he shook, and muttered to himself, and cried out in his sleep. Not that he had ever looked particularly happy, but now he seemed dismal. Morgan felt responsible.

Certain things had changed for the better, though. Meals were lavish now, for example: leg of lamb, juicy steak or sushi—never chicken, turkey, duck, or any kind of bird—mashed potatoes, vegetables, glistening desserts; they were profligate with pies. The one thing Zvominir saved money for was food, and Morgan paid attention to his cooking methods. Someday, when he was an expert in the kitchen, and when the RedBlacks were destroyed, he would cook for his father.

Drowsy with food, Morgan locked himself in his room, and dragged through a hole in the floor

to go meet Jane underground, where she would 1
make him read through documents, to help her
plot her revolution. Her paperwork and charts
were done in code—she had failsafed her endeavor
in so many different ways—which Morgan hadn't 5
learned, though he'd tried for, like, a day, but he
was sleepy and distracted, days were long, with all
the dangerous parts to come.

   She quizzed him on his reading, and he always scored poorly. Since when did rebels do 10
homework?

   Then would come the arson itself, where Jane
would be critical of everything he did. He left all
kinds of evidence behind—fire might destroy, but
not totally eradicate, the substances it touched— 15
and a smart forensic chemist could deduce what
had been burned, and trace it back to her, though
she always did her shopping in the tunnels,
bought ingredients from pearl-eyed bearded Gypsies whose green translucent luminescent skin be- 20
trayed a life with no exposure to the sun. Morgan
didn't take notes, didn't concentrate or learn, or
try to learn—where was his commitment to the
cause?—and stole objects that were vulgar, like
expensive clothes and shoes. Who the hell was he 25
trying to impress? She made him wear a shirt that
said *Rebels Don't Shop*.

   Morgan thought it might be hot to do it in the
building they were just about to burn, but Jane
grew cross and warned him not to sexualize the 30

fire. That's a totally different pathology, she said. We aren't perverts.

Finally, after all that, they fucked. Morgan fucked about as well as he arsoned, though Jane was, in this matter, more forgiving, and swore she loved that he was, in her words, trenchant. Her kindness was unbearable; at least when she was critical, he agreed with her. Intimacy tore from him a thing he couldn't name, and wished to keep. Call it self-respect. He grieved to learn that solitary sex surpassed his sex with Jane.

On his bird-route, he saw RedBlacks beating Gypsies on the street. Why do you do that, he asked Noah, who explained that they were looking for an arsonist, and did he, Morgan, have any leads to help the RedBlacks, his bodyguards and friends? Even if I did, Morgan said, I'd never tell you and you know it. If you did know, Noah said, and here he waved the bayonet he languourously sharpened in the sun until it gleamed, I could fucking make you sing.

Morgan stole a cookbook, and taught himself to cook. His specialty was Salmon Vesuvio, though he also liked the Vietnamese cuisine, cassoulets and bouillabaisses. He loved how normal cooking made him feel, how undramatic and domestic were the rites of cutting, mixing and waiting for the flame to do its work. He liked the sound of sizzling, he liked to pour a whole bottle of wine into a pot and let the meat soak it up in the oven.

In the tunnels, Gypsy boys weren't shy at rid-
iculing Jane, for some had previously dallied with
her. They had known her as a pacifist, and didn't
find her incarnation as a rebel credible. Some advanced this view to Morgan, who they idolized,
but did not understand in this instance. No, said
Morgan, she's for real; she's almost too real. He
almost added, I'm the fake. But she's crazy, said
the Gypsy boys, and they could not believe that
Morgan, with his power, would give his time to
her. Does she pester you, they asked. Is she hec-
toring and unpleasant? Does she make you do re-
search? Don't you hate taking orders from a girl?
She's a genius, Morgan said, which he believed,
for the most part, though of course he agreed that
she was difficult. If Jane was a guy, Morgan said,
quoting Jane, you'd never speak of her this way.
It was traitorous, he thought, to countenance a
Jane-bashing session, especially from Gypsies,
who she would lead to victory, if they weren't too
dense to follow.

He declared his loyalty to Jane, and said that
he would not permit attacks on her; that it was
he, Morgan, who had power over birds; he who,
the bird god, in his wisdom, had furnished with
the power, so the bird god must approve of Jane,
too. Further. It was Jane who had a plan, and the
Gypsy boys who lagged about the tunnels, smoking dope and listening to *ska*, polishing their pat-
ent leather shoes, and adding rhinestones to their

dreadlocks so they shimmered like the fountains in a mall, or practicing their instruments so they could play for money, instead of commandeering institutions, taking money for the Gypsy cause, and playing instruments for love. The boys admired his passion, and he came off as mysterious and focused. Get up off your ass and blow shit up, said Morgan, I command you.

And they listened, they were almost as obedient as birds. Soon, there wasn't just a single arsonist. There were dozens. On rooftops, he and Jane saw fires that weren't their own. RedBlacks captured these inferior Gypsy arsonists, or killed them, though some of them escaped, and cultivated grudges of their own, and fantasized of vengeance. They had been inspired.

24

Soldiers waited for Katherine to leave her school each afternoon. Her mother encouraged her to think of them as friends with guns, even though these friends were under orders not to talk to her. The guards set Katherine apart from her classmates, she who was already set apart, but now she had been doubly set apart, and there also loomed the hazard of her brother, whose reputation as a fiend didn't help her, either. No amount of protest changed her mother's mind; RedBlacks brought her home in a steel-plated carriage with an antique oak interior.

And so she hatched a plot, and smuggled a fancy dress inside her schoolbag for camouflage, and also stole a wig of long, blond hair from her school's performing arts facility, which allowed her to assimilate with classmates, for once. Thus could she escape the school unseen, and disappear into the streets.

Having achieved the first part of her plan, an accomplishment she didn't think was possible, and consequently hadn't thought beyond, she didn't know where she should go, and so she roamed the boulevards and watched the churning birdclouds overhead. She knew her mother would be panicked by this stunt.

Zvominir must be busy shifting birds, she thought, so she headed where she thought he would be. Birdclouds overhead didn't migrate, as birdclouds often did, but loitered, lazy as actual clouds. The black and sunless sky made her shiver, and the darkness of this light, the light of shadows, invoked her mother's bedroom, where chills lurked like grudges Katherine didn't understand.

But she didn't find the Swede man herding birds. It was Morgan.

There he was, in the front yard of a three-storey house with tall white pillars, his clothes scored with dirt and burn-marks. He was shockingly thin. She figured she might crush him with her cherishing, so fragile did he seem, and badly cared for. He needed the attention of a mother, or at least a girlfriend; the motherless, loveless, grubby, magic, gorgeous skinny boy whose shredded shirt revealed the V below his torso drove her wild with pity and desire. She would bathe him; she would wash his stomach; he would love her and need her.

RedBlacks sat in chairs beside a folding table half a block away, where they played cards. Katherine walked right up to him. She would show her mother.

What are you doing here, she asked.

25 Do I know you, he asked. He might as well have killed her! She felt so embarrassed she could barely say her name, but then he recognized her face. How had he not seen who she was!

You changed your hair, he said. She took off her wig, and said the dress was ugly, but a necessary ruse, and that she hated fancy clothes. He stopped himself from saying he had stolen that exact dress just three nights before, and had given it to Jane, who made him wear it, which worked out better than he cared to admit.

Morgan's escorts, incidentally, failed to recognize the Giggs girl. When they saw her with the wig on, they decided she was just another groupie and forgot about her.

Katherine explained that she wasn't allowed outside the house, and had resorted to disguises. My mom would kill me for talking to you, she said. I can't wait until she finds out. A lot of people use me as a tool of their rebellion, he said, quoting Jane. I'm not using you, she said. That's not what I meant, he said. Fuck, this is impossible, he thought. She thought the same thing.

Morgan said the RedBlacks weren't supposed to let him talk to anyone, but they were lazy, got drunk, ignored their jobs, so sometimes he could get away with it. Katherine was pleased, and Morgan perplexed, that they actually had something in common. She said she hated staying home, it drove her crazy, she had needed to get out. I didn't know the rich could be unhappy, he said. But we're miserable! she said. My mom never leaves her room except to kill flowers and yell at me, and my brother is crazy and won't do anything he's told. He's one of my biggest fans, Morgan said.

They laughed. The dress was more revealing than her usual clothes—he could see more of the round, smooth surface of delight that was her leg—and this encounter's informality gave her access to a repertoire of casual expressions he had never seen her use before. She was actually hot. And, despite the problem of communicating with her, she was still less difficult than Jane, and she had a sheepish, friendly smile that shyly blazed.

Still, he said, I'd like to have your money. No you wouldn't, she said. It's awful being rich. This she knew was a lie, it was great to be rich. She only said the opposite to impress him.

He said that if she knew how hungry people were in the city, she would never say such a thing. Even soup kitchens don't have any food. She should see them for herself. She blushed with shame. To be insensitive to him and his plight was not what she had wanted for this accidental meeting she had begged the gods to give her. It's okay, our thoughts are mediated by ideological state apparatuses, he said, quoting Jane again. By the way, he had never seen a soup kitchen, and he didn't know what ideological state apparatuses were, either. He could hardly pronounce them.

Katherine said she'd go read up. She showed her smile again, which, along with the fact that she was the daughter of the Judge, made her irresistible.

So you don't have anywhere to be right now, he asked. Nope, she said, I'm just waiting for someone to notice I'm gone. He made a table and two chairs out of crows, candlesticks of hummingbirds, and chickadee candles. The flames were swirling orioles and cardinals. He even formed a man who played a violin, though, because the violin was made of birds, it made no music. In addition, there were problems with the scale of this particular composition. Morgan usually rendered images in the sky, where they could be huge, but these were on the street and right beside him and Katherine, normal-sized and unconvincing. Katherine rubbed her eyes, for she did not understand what she saw. What am I looking at, she said.

He had never been asked this question, had never failed even remotely to elicit gaping awe. He explained what objects he'd portrayed. Oh, she said. You're taking me out to dinner. She walked a lap around the table and said, It's good, in, like, a modern-art kind of way. Fake encouragement felt worse to him than insults. You rich suburban girls are ruthless, he said.

Next, he made a man who chased a wind-blown hat down the street. Whenever the bird-made-man thought he had it, the hat slipped away. This I understand, she said. It's the human condition. Let's hope it's not a symbol for this seduction, Morgan said. Are you seducing me, she asked. I hadn't noticed.

This was a lie; of course she'd noticed. She was thrilled. Still, she figured she should make him work at least a little, and show some pride in these, the final moments before she threw herself at him. Morgan winced and said, You really are your father's daughter. And you, she said, are impetuous in daring to seduce the Judge's favorite child. How brave. I'm not afraid of anything, he said. I'm famous for that.

He made her face-of-birds in the sky. That's more like it, she said. Narcissist, he said. You're the one who's pandering, she said. You're the one who's just like everyone else, he said. Now it was Katherine's turn to wince. You can take the girl out of the suburbs, he continued, but you can't take the suburbs out of the girl. Can you insult me using something other than clichés? Excuse me for not having your private school education, I've been busy defending the oppressed.

The portrait of her face transformed into her body, and she was in a haberdashery, trying on hats. Of the rows of hats of birds that Morgan made, she preferred the one with cherries, grapes and apricots sprouting from the band. Kind of a kooky old lady hat, he said. The hat the crazy cat lady wears. The lady who always lives on her own terms, Katherine said.

A chariot heaped with RedBlacks came hammering down the street. The newly arrived, unusually sober soldiers asked the drunken, listless soldiers if they'd seen the Giggs girl anywhere. That must be my ride, Katherine said. When will I see you again, he asked. He was desperate: he had tried to snare her heart, but she'd seized his instead. She said her mom would never let her out after this. She felt desperate, too, and while this sweet and brief encounter would be played out in her mind for a hundred lonely nights, she wanted it again, and for real.

26

And that's when RedBlacks beat the shit out of him.

RedBlacks had gone searching for the daughter of the Judge, who had vanished after school. Hundreds of them hit the streets in carriages, and they didn't gallop far before they knew where they were going: to the center of the sun-blotting birdcloud, where Katherine's face-in-birds was afloat, like a lotus in water. Morgan accidentally made her face with his mind. This was what the RedBlacks had feared: she'd been hijacked by the Bird Boy! It was danger! They rushed to Katherine's rescue, found her wearing clothes they had never seen her dress in. She looked almost normal, and was standing by the Bird Boy, about to be attacked. He had probably worked some kind of Gypsy-hoodoo curse on her or something.

Morgan had this beatific look on his face, like some kind of fanatic, as if to say, *Beat me, I don't care*. So they obliged. Don't hurt him, she cried, but the RedBlacks didn't listen. They hurt him. They liked hurting Morgan. Bodyguarding people was boring, torture was amusing, passed the time, and gratified them, somehow. It must be good if it feels good.

They knocked him down and kicked him with

their boots, which Katherine tried to stop, but soldiers held her back, as they said later, under questioning, for her own safety. They might've kept kicking him all night if Katherine hadn't wriggled from the chokehold and scrambled toward the crowd of Morgan-beaters, shoving and forcing her way to the boy, and diving on his body to protect him, and she may have saved his life, he had started coughing blood. He saw that she had saved him.

You people are animals, she told the Red-Blacks. *I hate you.*

2 7 What the Judge really wished to do, as he set out to mollify his daughter, was torture Morgan with a cheese-grater, make him squeal in agony, then kill him. This would be impossible, alas; he needed the powers of the Bird Boy and his father. But just because he couldn't do it wouldn't stop him from imagining. He was often torn between worlds this way: half of him in reverie for what he'd do in private, and half marooned in reality.

He would string the Bird Boy's arms above his head, let him hang there in the cold, ice him down with freezing water. He would whip him, break his bones, let them heal, break them all again. He would put the boy in a drawer, and never let him out, hold him down on a table and pour water on his face until the boy thought he would drown. He would frame the boy for arson, for the birds, for being gay. He would fuck him up the ass with a broomstick.

Katherine had proudly displayed her split lip to her classmates and mother, tearing off the bandage and flaunting her ruby-looking scabs, the treasures of her courage. The Judge worried for his Katherine, who didn't seem to know which side she was on in the scrape between the Red-Blacks and Morgan—leave it to a girl to misinter-

pret power, politics, and every other thing—and
yet, admired how she'd dived into the fray to
save the Bird Boy. She was braver than Mike, and
both smarter and dumber. The Judge climbed
the white steps to her room. The idea of bicker-
ing with Katherine made him anxious, but he
tried to find it charming. He seldom actually had
to fight these days, and always got his way before
a conflict reached the point of someone hazard-
ing a disagreement with him. The years since the
war had been good, at least until the advent of the
birds and the Gypsies, and those fucking Gypsy
Swedes.

Katherine was his darling, and her courage,
however foolishly misplaced, proved why he loved
her. Charlie had never been the favorite, though
it had helped politically to act as if he was, after
the fact. The city could relate to a father who had
lost his son in war, it made them love the Giggs
clan at a moment when the city had to sacrifice,
and helped the Judge look valiant to his soldiers.
His first-born's merits had emerged a bit in retrospect. Charlie had pronounced awkward words in
a fine way, for example, and how had he learned
that? He could've said "Zvominir." And he was a
natural musician. Mike shared his love of music,
though he didn't have the talent. Katherine was
sweet and unspoiled, like her father wanted her to
be. He didn't want to deal with someone else like
her mother.

Narrative carpets were silent underfoot, and illustrated triumphs-in-tableaux. Many of the heroes portrayed there were his forbears, and the presence of their stories reassured him. When something went wrong in the city, he played it down and found someone to blame, who he purged, and so enforced his authority; when something went wrong in his family, he enforced his authority by not discussing it. This taught his family to forget, or to keep it themselves. Yes, he had regrets, who didn't? Now was not the time to talk about them. That time would be never.

His wife had taken up religion. Monks were coming over every afternoon for tea. She was chasing absolution for Charlie. There was only so much of that the Judge could take. He arrived at Katherine's door.

Or he could torture Zvominir, and make Morgan watch, or torture Morgan and make Zvominir watch, or torture them both at the same time. Katherine sat on the floor and fed a parrot from her hand. He tried to pay attention. She glared, who did not know the purpose of a glare: to threaten, which Katherine could not do, she had no power. The talking birds appeared to have nested here for good, and even if he burned his house down, which he'd fantasized about, they probably would huddle by the ashes, squawk triumphantly and call out Charlie's name, to rub it in.

Katherine frowned around her ruined lip.

Boastfully, he thought. The men who had done this to her face had been made into examples. No one touched his Katherine, or let her get away. Yes, she had been wrong to dive into the pile, but she was right in her wrongness, born as this wrongness was of the noblest intentions. Courage in women, he mused. It could be dangerous.

You don't approve of the parrots, Katherine said. Truthfully, he said, I never gave it a thought. Do your soldiers always beat up innocent people? He assured her they didn't, in the sweetest possible voice, and said he stood against pain, and would mobilize his wisdom and experience to stop its use forever. I hope you do, she said, It's inhuman. You're supposed to be in charge, can't you make your soldiers act nicer? Being a soldier is a difficult job, he said. Sometimes they have to use force, it's a dangerous world, which of course you wouldn't know, my little pet, safe and snug here as you are. But Morgan wasn't hurting anybody. The men thought you might be in danger, Gypsies are unpredictable. But he's not a Gypsy. Whatever the hell he is, they were just being careful, and it turns out he'll be fine in two or three weeks, so there's nothing to worry about, no harm done; no lasting harm, anyway, nothing that will hurt beyond a month or two. He helplessly imagined what an actual beating would have looked like. Morgan doesn't know what a real beating is, said the Judge, and, for that matter, neither do you.

Why do you think Gypsies are dangerous, she asked. Because you beat them all the time. Was there ever a greater exaggeration, he smiled. You truly are your mother's daughter. We don't beat Gypsies, sweetie. A couple bad seeds accidentally kicked Morgan because they thought you were in trouble, which, if you hadn't sneaked out of school, they wouldn't have had any reason to think that, now would they?

I'm bored, she said. I hate that I get hurried home after school. I'm not in any danger, nothing's dangerous here. He saw how she preened, that she prepared to flex some victim muscle. Of course it's not dangerous here, that's by design. It isn't fair, Mike can do whatever he wants, he doesn't even have to go to school. He had given Katherine everything she'd wanted in this world, had pried it from the cold, dead hands of those who'd had it first. What do you want that you don't have, he asked. I want to work with Gypsies in the city, she said.

Excuse me?

I want to do charity, she said. For the needy. Say that again, he said; he'd been picturing Morgan and Zvominir bent over chairs. She said it again, and she looked so engaged, almost obsessed, while he could hardly pay attention. Your mother will love that, he said. The city is filled with suffering people, she continued, and I want to help them. Thoughts are mediated by ideological state apparatuses, you know. He knew all too well, which is why he controlled them. How do you propose to help them exactly, since they refuse to help themselves? I could feed them, she said, or give them medicine, or teach them how to read. Okay, he said. I'll arrange it. But you'll have to show up and work like everybody else. There won't be any preferential treatment. This, of course, was a lie; aid workers weren't surrounded by soldiers, as Katherine would be. I want to be like everybody else, she said, I want to be normal. That's never going to happen, he said, which made her frown, as if some aspect of her precious self-image had been ruined. The things kids bitch about these days.

I'm sick of being a prisoner in this house, she continued, gathering herself to issue more complaints. Fine, he said, interrupting her and bored, all of a sudden, with this charade of a concession. He would find a way to make this come out in his favor, just you wait. On Monday, after school, he said, you can go downtown to a soup kitchen. He was chewing on his lip, his cheeks, his tongue and any flesh along the inside of his mouth his teeth could cling to. Katherine helping Gypsies! It was all too much, really.

You think I'm going to quit, she said. You think I'll do the job for one day and decide I don't like it and quit. You think I'm some kind of phony.

I love you more than ever, you're my master-
piece, he said.

She shook her head and stood, with a motion
and a doubt he had never seen before, because
she'd just discovered it.

I don't buy this, she said. You don't buy what?
This. This conversation. How calm you are. I think
you're patronizing me, I think this whole exchange
has been you telling me what I want to hear. Have
you been talking to your mother, asked the Judge.
No, said Katherine. You know I haven't, you know
I'm nothing like her. Don't change the subject.

You're getting what you want, aren't you, he
said. Yes. Then don't ask any more fucking questions. You might not like the answers.

He left the room; he could not torture who
he wanted. He told his men to gather up some
Gypsies and some livestock, and bring them, in
chains, to his office in the city, or better yet, the
chamber in the basement of the coach house near
the Giggs house gate, which RedBlacks used as
place of recreation, and where no one in his family was allowed. The Judge would henceforth call
this room The BoomBoom Room.

28 RedBlacks redeployed throughout the city, to stop the arsons, but the fires couldn't be predicted. Soldiers knew the man who planned the fires must be better than all the other Gypsies they had faced. Fuck, they thought, the *untermensch* evolved. The tutor had been on the case for weeks, to no avail; he'd actually been vanquished by a Gypsy. The very best RedBlack had been spit back in the face of the Judge. Every night, the soldiers fanned out in the pattern of a snowflake, and every night, buildings burned.

A letter arrived to the Judge. It contained a code for the arsons which combined addresses of the buildings which had burned, and a key for transposing numbers into letters. The tutor followed the instructions, and came up with a sentence:

You are going down.

29 The neighborhood surrounding the soup kitchen Katherine would work at needed to be safe. The Judge sent his RedBlacks to cleanse the zone of Gypsies, young men, skinny girls, laggards, dirty-looking arsonist suspect-types, or anybody else who looked too innocent.

When all of the apartments had been vacated, and Gypsies had been thrashed and dumped in other neighborhoods, Mike and the tutor arrived. The tutor thought that actual apartments would be useful in teaching Mike the skills of a RedBlack, and, since there happened to be streets of empty buildings now, why not make the tenements an authentic simulacrum of slums? Why not teach Mike in a city, with its smells of crime and poverty? Plus, he wouldn't have to make all his mistakes at The RedBlack Academy, where everyone could see him fail. He could be concealed, and, when he wasn't stupid anymore, revealed anew. The Judge agreed. Mike would learn in the city. The notion of teaching Mike in such a place, the homes of blameless, disenfranchised Gypsies, was dreadful to the tutor, which made him recommend it. Morally atrocious ideas always got the best reactions from his bosses.

Mike was dispatched to emptied apartments

near the soup kitchen, the tutor going with him and quizzing him in B&E's, shakedowns, interrogating suspects, and searching out forbidden hidden weapons. The Gypsies who had lived in these new pedagogical facilities had looked tired and desperate; the tutor couldn't bear to think of them. The tutor taught Mike to kick down doors, how to check the corners and closets and bedrooms, how to hold his rifle and his pistol, and when to use the bayonet. For now, he just used dummies. The tutor showed Mike how to question suspects, and how to sniff out what was hidden. Minor tips sometimes led to major ones, he said; even the slightest hint of information could help you catch rebels. Search under carpets and inside every drawer, box and pocket, cabinet and pantry, said the tutor. You have to learn to conjugate a Gypsy into evidence; the quest is epistemological, insofar as we can never know enough, can never truly know what we know, or know our unknowns. Whatever, Mike thought, As long as I kick some ass.

They worked on the fine points of smashing teeth with gun-butts; Mike took to it immediately. Investigative work, like all sports, rewarded winners. It was just another game, Mike figured, and the city was his playing field.

Thoughts of Katherine caused the tutor misery. She clearly didn't like him, and would've been enraged if she'd known that Gypsies suffered just to make it safe for her to help them. He'd spoken to her just the other day, beneath a spruce that drooped with parrots, like ripe and talking fruit. He'd asked about her wound, which she'd gleefully explained to be the work of RedBlack monsters just like him. Then she stomped toward a bank of delphinium, basking in the aura of her dis. In her way, she was crueler than her brother. But I'm not a monster, he insisted, catching up to her, I'm a teacher and a poet. You're teaching my brother to beat people up. I'm teaching him to govern, he's young, and just likes the violent parts, patience comes slowly to boys, we aren't as thoughtful or generous as girls, except of course for some of us, like me. He could see that this encounter, which he'd practiced many times in his head, had veered utterly off course, and yet he understood her suspicion. Should he tell her that punishment guaranteed obedience? That force, and force alone, made people co-exist in peace, that peace could only flourish under threat? That peace could fail? I heard you're doing charity, he said. Katherine nodded, saying, Someone has to heal the wounds you cause.

He bowed and withdrew, fled the estate, and made for the whorehouse. He admired little Katherine, detested himself, toiled with her disapproval's specter at night, in the arms of his hooker, where he fucked but failed to sleep, sneezing in the smog of crappy perfume. The girl-for-hire

didn't like his poems; her parents had been professors; she knew talent when she saw it, or at last
she thought she did. The war had orphaned her,
and she'd been sold to this harem; her johns were
distinguished and few. The tutor often cried in the
arms of this girl, who made him pay extra. Most
of her clients cried, she said. Many didn't even
want to fuck, only to be held. Should I even think
of prostitutes this way, he wondered. He knew he
treated them as clichés.

He had hoarded mental images of Katherine
to use during sex, and yet, amid the act, he could
not recall her face. He remembered dates, places,
quotes and philosophical ideas, but never Katherine's face, his mind a kind of ramshackle crammed
with so many useless notions, while hers, he supposed, was an origami library, fragile and pure.
His days seemed dark and lonesome unless he
saw her, his nights were days for brightness when
she came to him in dreams; he could not recall his
dreams. He handed her a chapbook of his poems,
and she didn't say she'd read them.

Mike began enjoying his trips into the city
with the tutor. Although he was a weakling, he was
interesting company, and knew about the battles
that had raged on all the streets, the men who had
died there, and what exact strategic blunders or
plain bad luck had led them to their deaths. The
guy seemed to take a strange, disproportionate
pleasure in studying failure, and he seldom spoke

of triumph. He knew the names of all the officers who'd made these wrong decisions, and who'd been victimized by chance or crappy weather. Internalize this stuff, said the tutor, then forget it. Hopefully it washes back in waves when you need it. Then he would talk about how memory worked. Then he would talk about how neurons worked. Then he would talk about how liquor worked, and why to avoid it, or how much to drink if you indulged, a little was enough, it took the edge off, but just what was this edge? Then he talked about The Eye of the Tiger, which had something to do with this goop in the brain that combined with other goop. It all came down to if you were depressed, said the tutor, or prone to depression. One should be positive, determined, and swift to adjust, though most are incapable and dwell in their own patterns, which are mazes made of habits, where all paths lead to gloom. Then he would go silent for a while, and his face would get sad. He was thinking about Katherine. Everybody knew he was in love with her, though no one knew why. Mike had his own ideas: Katherine was fucked in the head, and the tutor liked things you could never figure out, stuff you could talk about forever, without reaching a conclusion.

The tutor failed teaching Mike the beliefs of the Gypsies, perhaps because he found no logic there, for Gypsy holy stories can't be read as anything but a montage of human desperation.

Gypsies draw belief from sundry sacred ancient books, where kings and con men play out narratives of failure, rape, murder, war, revenge and sodomy. Every fifty pages, a bird emerges from the earth, sings a prophecy in birdspeak, and flees for the sky, leaving landborne mortals to interpret cryptic chirps. The oracle-interpreters act on their desires, and, unless their god, a kind of bird-and-human hybrid, likes them, they screw up, and more catastrophe ensues. Our own holy text is more or less the same—though we don't have the birds, or a bird god—and our lives are also pretty much the same, though we don't have an oracle to tell us what to do. Possibly disaster is the oracle, but how should we respond to disaster? What does ruin say, but we've been fools before, and shall be again? The tutor knew that sacred books can be uncanny.

Gypsies had their holidays and rituals. Most involve dressing up as birds, running, flapping, and dancing to devotional rock-steady. *Ska* is ritualized music, for birds like to dance. Prayers are spoken every day, and in the evening. Monday is the Sabbath, which explains at least in part why Gypsies can't get jobs, except in restaurants: they simply do not work Mondays. Once a month, Gypsies celebrate by fasting, and flagellate themselves.

Day after day, Mike stormed into buildings and beat up training dummies. He got impatient.

The tutor said that maybe Mike would learn more if the band didn't follow them everywhere, but Mike said, Fuck that. The tutor shrugged, and followed with a speech on how the city's arsonist should really be called an *arsonista*: someone who could actually transform their inchoate rage into intelligence, with fire as the product.   The only part of inchoate Mike got was hate.

Mike often ditched the tutor for his band. His clarinet lessons with Chico would begin with shots of liquor, and when the Gypsies started running and thumping out their *ska*, Mike would try and fail to keep up. The band, led by Chico, would run backwards and taunt him as they played, and encourage him with words such as fuckbreath. They would wave their liquor bottles overhead, chant in rhythm, and demand he play along, which of course he could not do, but it was joy to fail at this. They ran along the shore, in every suburb, and through half the city's restaurants, Chico giving pointers all the time, telling him to jog, then to sprint, then to skip, then to hop, and never stop his playing. Mike played music in his dreams now.

Then it was back to his lessons. The tutor was Talmudic on this *arsonista* person. When he'd first been told to catch him, he figured it would take him two weeks; a month at most. But now he knew that he would have to just get lucky. The *arsonista* used a formula that could not be predicted, he said. The pattern looked like snowflakes, but deployed random elements to subvert any possible calculation. The tutor didn't feel upset that he had lost to a Gypsy, which Mike, who always had to win at everything, found odd. It's not that I'm not competitive, said the tutor, though I'm not, which is why I'm not a famous soldier, and why I teach. It's that the person setting fires is a genius, who no mode of prediction can catch, his imagination is too generous. Imagination is everything. I'll tell you something else, but you should keep this to yourself, it'll make me look crazy. The *arsonista* takes no sexual pleasure in setting fires, and he's too steady to be a younger man. Unless I'm generalizing stupidly, it's a woman. We're losing to a woman.

30 Morgan spent his recovery in the apartment while his father did double-time de-birding, dragging feathered tendrils through the sky like smokestack smoke attached to rope. His body was a giant purple bruise, more a spoiled skinny root than the prison of a ghost, and he coughed and shat blood. He didn't leave his bedroom, except to climb onto his rooftop late at night, to watch the stubborn fires whose light would not go out. Night, he thought, the time of plots and sneaking, though maybe plots could be more dangerous in the day, without night's cloak of anonymity. Maybe the night was more honest, in the sense that it openly concealed things, as opposed to the day, which concealed by pretending to reveal.

He thought a lot about lying; he lied to Jane all the time. She didn't know of Katherine's role in his beating; he claimed he'd earned it by insulting his RedBlack guards. Jane was so proud she called him her hero, and she could not stop kissing him. She couldn't see the truth, because she looked with admiration's foolish eyes. She couldn't see that Katherine had overthrown his thoughts.

With Zvominir at work, Jane lounged in Morgan's bedroom, insofar as it was comfortable to do so, and read from the newspaper. *The arson was the latest in an apparently ongoing series, though officials say arrests are imminent.* They don't know who they're searching for, she said, looking smug. Good thing, said Morgan. He felt decidedly unsmug, with all his injuries, but she said this was progress: the figurehead had finally been brave, and the press was on board. Forward!

Jane had stopped walking on the street. She stayed underground. The surface was too dangerous.

Anyone who braved the streets at night to taunt RedBlacks disappeared for days, reappearing later, looking shattered. Morgan understood why the RedBlacks beat people: how else could crime be discouraged? He didn't blame them for trying to stop the fires, he wouldn't want to lose his own possessions, if he ever got some worth keeping. He also felt the pride that came from work, which Jane did not approve of, she had never had a job. The night before, he'd stood beside her on his rooftop, where flames shone in the distance. Dozens of other Gypsies started fires. It was wrong. There had to be another, better way.

The plan, she said, had worked. It's amazing, they're following our lead. But Morgan didn't want to lead, if this was what his leading led to. Yes, he was angry he'd been beaten, angry he was poor and a second-class citizen, angry he'd been angry all his life, but this firestarting business seemed dumb, and doomed to fail, unless the goal was just to burn, in which case it succeeded, but what kind of goal was that, to blow shit up for no reason? He was scared. He hated fire, yet he spread it through the city. What had he begun? The flames seemed like nothing more than camp-fires in the distance, too weak to heat his face. And yet, he counted nineteen fires, in a time of total lockdown. Gypsies risked their lives to set them.

He thought all of it was wrong.

Jane brought Morgan feasts she'd stolen, and giant bags of get-well-soon cards she'd collected in the tunnels. You have so many fans, she said. I'm proud of you. She'd planned her life around him, and he never said a word to dissuade her. He promised he would stand beside her through it all: the escalating violence and the war that sure-ly followed; all the losses they'd accrue, and the city they would build in Billy's honor. He hadn't meant a word of it. He didn't want a revolution, and yet he was responsible for one, and for her. He wanted Katherine Giggs.

In the morning, his father shined his shoes, to prepare for de-birding. Suburban clients liked impeccable employees. He pinned a boutonnière to his lapel, a frilly surface flower so unlike the sewer's nightplants. Morgan objected to the bou-tonniere's politics. He'd insisted to his father he was innocent, but the Bird Man blamed him for the beating. That's just like you, Morgan said, to listen to their story over mine, you're so damn condescending, I'm the one who got attacked, why don't you listen to me?

Does Jane know Katherine was involved, Zvominir asked. Have you told her?

Who told you, Morgan asked.

RedBlacks. Don't be stupid. They were thrilled to let me know that they might yet get the chance to beat you to death.

Crap, Morgan said.

If you can't look out for yourself, said his father, no one will. The city wants you dead. Please, he said, don't provoke them into killing you, you're the only thing I love that still exists.

What about the birds, Morgan asked.

Birds piss me off, he said, I just want to be normal.

He didn't know his father had been trying to enroll him in reputable schools in the suburbs. Zvominir had learned in his travels through the suburbs that the city had improbably large numbers of integrated Gypsies, who'd come many generations ago, and assimilated, somehow. The Bird Man couldn't solve the mystery of an entrance application, and RedBlacks who escorted him had lied when he had asked for help, to make certain he would fail. When he finally sent the applications in, they were rejected out of hand, without an explanation. Letters he had written asking why his son had been denied went unanswered, and nobody would meet with him. Zvominir would have worked all day and night and never slept, he would have taken Morgan's shifts on his bird-route; he would have done anything. He labored to be harmless and dependable. But no suburban school admitted Morgan.

31 Monks had been visiting Mrs. Giggs. They arrived dressed in robes of white and red, bowing to everyone they met and unnerving them. The Judge did not feel comfortable near monks, who had once been normal people, except weaker, and therefore somehow threatening. But his wife had invited them, welcomed them into her room, knelt and prayed with them, met with them every few days, dropped their leaflets in the corners of the house as hints to her family, filled the air with incense, and her children's ears with stories of religion. The monks had come from The Cloister, a spiritual facility atop a mountain. At The Cloister, monks spent their lives in silent meditation. Because these were difficult times, many fled to The Cloister, or tried to, admission was difficult, though it wouldn't be hard for Mrs. Giggs, whose husband would offer to explode it if they didn't take his wife. The Cloister offered hope that the miseries of life could vanish with devotion to God.

Those who fled to The Cloister to study with the monks were seldom seen again, unless we visited them there. We weren't allowed to speak during visits, though at first we didn't mind, stunned as we were by the beauty of The Cloister, and the oddness of our loved ones. Footpaths lined by fences of stone traced the fogged rims of peaks, curtains of lush and brilliant colors swayed in the wind, which seemed the very breath of God, though God traffics not in vulgar matter, He made the world as we know it as a shield to hide Himself, and withdrew to a place outside the world, and although we do not understand the characteristics of this not-place, we have only to feel the beauty of The Cloister spreading out within our souls to know that there is something more than knowing.

The final day of visits to our loved ones on The Cloister included an entreaty from the non-Cloister spouse to sneak off to a trail and actually speak of fallen things, such as children, jobs, and mortgages. Weekends without talking and with meals of food which tasted, how shall we say, subtle, had made the non-believers into skeptics. When are you coming home, they asked. Never, their spouses replied. I will never leave The Cloister.

Those who lived in the village at the foot of Mount Cloister described a stream of gloomy spouses who rode down on donkeys, muttering divorce. Did the Judge see such a future donkey ride? Probably not. Probably, he wanted his wife to leave the house, so he wouldn't have to have her around. Did his children see a misty ride of grief on a donkey in the future? This, too, is unlikely; children weren't allowed on The Cloister. Did Katherine and Mike want their mother gone to a monastery? The truth cannot be said in words. Would you want your mother to leave? If she was miserable, would you want to her to be happy? Even if it meant she had to leave you, never see you again?

32 Mike, Tom and Gus joined the band at a barbecue, deep inside the city. Their RedBlack escort detail numbered over fifty, and the tutor felt petrified exposing Mike this way, so far in hostile territory, but Mike could not be budged from his plans. Chico promised all the great musicians of the city would be there, so Mike should bring his clarinet. I'm not good enough, he said, I'll embarrass myself. That's right, Chico said, you suck, you're a pussy. He playfully swung his instrument at Mike, and chased him, and both of them laughed.

Chico was a tall, bent-up Gypsy as big as a door, who looked like a fire-scored tree. He was also a virtuoso on the clarinet. Chico didn't know his own age—no birth certificate existed—but the tutor put him near sixty. He possessed all the knowledge, stories, classic dirty jokes, and seemingly authentic old-world wisdom Mike had lately found he craved. Chico's life was drinking, having fun, playing *ska*, and he never, never once, yelled at Mike. He also never mentioned Charlie's name, and probably hadn't even heard of him. Mike was Chico's favorite Giggs, and the only Giggs he cared about. Mike was not a disappointment to him.

Chico's clarinet instruction was unserious, for he never seriously criticized his student, and only joked around. He had no real responsibility for Mike, unlike the tutor, whose anxieties were vast. The tutor felt jealous. Mike and Chico were friends, while he was left to do his job and not be loved.

The barbecue took place in what passed for a park in this slum: a rubble-strewn lot with banks of weeds tall and dense, where pits had been dug into the earth for use as ovens, and goals made of burned-up carriages marked soccer fields of stone. Towering public housing surrounded this so-called park, and snipers could be anywhere. The tutor demanded the party be cancelled; Red-Blacks could never cleanse the area of threats, but Mike said not to sweat it, and dismissed these concerns with a wave of his ignorant, pseudo-royal hand. The Gypsy musicians who had gathered with their families were likewise scared: of Mike and his RedBlacks, but Chico assured them that Mike was not a threat. So they all came out to meet him.

Mike would interact with the Gypsies in the only way that mattered: a game of soccer. Mike's team had the children of the band, and any other kids who showed up; the other team had grownups. Gypsies were second only to Mancunians in their greatness at soccer, and Mike could never hope to match their skill, but he re-contextualized the game into a battle of endurance, and led the children, who could run forever, to a win against

the adults, who they wore out with their hunting
of the ball, with their youth and the sheer exuber-
ance he inspired in them. He made himself the
captain, and he led, and made all kinds of moti-
vating speeches, complete with jokes and obscenities, which the Gypsy kids loved.

For dinner, Mike partook of that glorious
Gypsy delicacy, the awesome contribution to the
culinary arts of the world: the bacon cheeseburger. Chico's grandsons taught Mike how to cook it,
and when they were done, he carried them around
on his back, and raced other Gypsies, who also
carried children on their backs. Tom and Gus did
it, too, and so did many RedBlacks, who drained
two kegs.

The tutor didn't join the games, and skipped
the bacon cheeseburger. He liked to feel left out,
and the fringes of the party, which he lurked, were
the best place to find the *arsonista*, if she was really here, though somebody that smart would
know that it was crazy to show her face to all those
RedBlacks. Still, the urge would be hard to resist,
even for someone as considered as her.

He could see the fires that blossomed in the
distance, so maybe she exploited how Mike's
visit to the ghetto left the city even more under-
manned. Tricky Gypsy. After the races and the
beer, the band took up their instruments. Gypsies of all ages joined in; the tutor counted almost
two hundred of them. They spontaneously ran,

and Mike tried to join them, though he still could hardly play when he was standing, let alone at a gallop. Guitarists and bassists carried amps on their backs. Mike asked Chico, How in hell did you people learn to do this? We're always running from something, Chico said, now mind your circular breathing. In through the nose, and out the mouth, like I told you.

Unlike his tutor, Mike had no trouble blending in. In the presence of *ska* and soccer, he seemed to forget he hated Gypsies. He was young enough to think the feeling music gave him actually meant something, and maybe it did, for look at the effect it had. He would probably choose music over military service. How would that preference be received by the Judge? The tutor hoped he'd never find out.

We could use *ska* to unite the bitter halves of the city, thought the tutor; hold a concert in the Giggs' back yard for the Gypsies and the Judge, cook some bacon cheeseburgers, make of everybody's anger a friendship that would last, instead of passively submitting to the war that seemed to loom, and would cost so many lives, etc. What a hippyish and stupid idea, thought the tutor. It embarrassed him to think it.

As the party broke up, the tutor spoke to Chico. Tell me, he said. How come no one tried assassinating Mike?

We certainly had offers to that effect, said

Chico. But we rejected them. Killing him here would be dishonorable, and Gypsies are an honorable people. Mike is just misunderstood, and we think he'll make a better, more sympathetic leader than his father. We like him, he's a really great kid. You guys have him wrong.

33

Our children wore accessories that featured Morgan's image; we purchased them at escalating prices. Gypsies sold these objects, at first, until the Judge muscled in, after which the Gypsies paid a tribute, or, as the Judge called it, an entertainment tax, or as we called it, good business, or, as the Gypsies called it, extortion.

We didn't know why the Bird Boy had been injured, the papers said an accident, implying it had been his fault. All of us wanted him back at work de-birding, many of us wanted him dead. Our children sent him cards that read *Get Well, We Miss You!*, or suchlike sentiments, which they'd made during school. At recess, the children mimicked Gypsy dances, spinning on their heads like Jewish toys. Some of them even started *ska* bands. We found our offspring helplessly enthralled by Gypsy culture. It was out of control. What were our suburbs coming to, and where was the outrage?

The get-well cards disappeared into the ghetto, kind of like our taxes. For all we cared, the Bird Boy burned the cards. Why had God cursed us with birds, and worse, with only Gypsies to de-bird us, or Swedes, or whatever they were called? Had we been punished for our sins, and, if so, which sins?

The war with Hungary? That bit about how Hungary attacked us, for example: it isn't really true. We pretty much provoked them. There were really persuasive reasons for it. No one can judge us who wasn't there, it's more than a you-had-to-be-there thing; it's a you-had-to-feel-our-fear thing, for when so many bodies feel the fear, can they still be held responsible? Our memory would speak about our guilt, and our pride would shout it down, kind of thing. God liked to talk about our guilt, however, and the birds were his words, and so were Gypsies, that red-haired, pock-marked pox upon our city.

We suspected, in our hearts, that we deserved the birds.

The Bird Boy we hated but needed like a maid who knows our house more than we do went back to his birds, herding flocks into sky-blotting thunderheads and sending them to migrate to the forests, until they changed their stupid bird-minds, or instinct called them back, or whatever it was that happened, don't ask us, we still don't understand, there aren't enough of us to be an "us" anymore. We are obsolete. The Swedes took the same routes as the garbage men, which is really what they were to us: specialists in garbage. Mystic, feathered garbage. They even kept the same schedules as the garbagemen; the actual garbage collectors toiled in their wake.

The birdshows, the feathery ineffable, re-

sumed, after nine barren days. Once again, we
trooped into the city with our children, though
time had already made us doubtful of our memories. We hoped the boy had lost whatever powers he had had; we tried to pretend he'd never
had them. His performances were some kind of
mistake, we insisted, and set about renouncing
them.

But once we saw the birdshows again, our resistance to his art disappeared. The thrill we had
forgotten grew stronger, we were rapt against our
will, our awe unwelcome, our appetite the hun-
grier the more we disavowed it. The boy himself
was camouflaged in bruises, we could hardly see
his gestures in the shadows of the square, his face
seemed smeared by violets. The birds, ah, you
birds, we could see you in the sunset. You made
your own sunset. The sun, blushing, hurried off
the stage, bested by the birds and the Bird Boy. He
somehow used finches to out-gold the gold of the
sun. Stars made of snowbirds seemed to wink in
the nightblack of crows. Who could help but weep
before his palette? It had never been more beautiful, yet he limped across the square, wounded
from the beating.

34

Morgan found his bird-route had been changed. He had traded, without knowing why, the ghetto for the fancy, leafy neighborhoods he'd veered near before, but never entered. The new route was pleasant, the limpid sky and grass left him enchanted. He liked being distant from his father, Jane, and all the other aspects of his life: the fires and claustrophobia, the muggy swampy wetness of the tunnels which had soaked his clothes forever, the simple lack of green and blue, and anything but gray. He liked to leave his neighborhood, and hated going back to it. Why am I a Swede, he wondered, not a placid country-dweller?

He even performed little birdshows for the children who lined the streets, and kicked a soccer ball with them, too. The Gypsyesque clothes of these kids surprised him; pricey-looking, fashionable knockoffs of ghetto-dweller fashion, the type of clothes he hated, and yet he had to wear them, for they were what he owned apart from what he'd stolen and could not wear in public, for fear of being outed as a thief. The kids liked his clothes and asked him where he got them. I fished them out of garbage cans, he said. You're so cool, they said. I'll trade you, he said, and they traded on the street. He actually saw *ska* bands at practice in garages. He could not resist the admiration of these bands, for they dedicated songs to him. Some of them wore shirts that bore his face, and they even baked him cookies. The quiet awe of customers, the rides through the fields, the solitude, the healing of his wounds—the pain was mostly gone—he actually felt happy. He dreaded coming back to the city, where Jane wouldn't understand.

His workday consisted of encounters with boys who thought he was cool, and girls who clustered on driveways and smiled at him, sexy and intrigued. Many asked to meet him after birdshows. They promised they'd stay out all night to see him, and would give him a night he would never forget. Even his RedBlack escorts mellowed when they saw he could be friendly. An atmosphere of festivals prevailed.

All this good cheer allowed the RedBlacks to drink on the job without fear of mishap. They told him they liked him. We'd heard you were surly, they said, but you're actually charming. We see why the Judge moved your bird-route away from his daughter.

What are you talking about, he asked.

They told him his bird-route had been altered because Katherine was working in a soup kitchen after school, spooning free glop to starving Gypsies. The Judge wants to keep you away from the girl, they said.

The next day, on his bird-route, he set out

to scare suburban customers, and get his route diverted back to the city, to be closer to Katherine. He swirled the birds into tornadoes, and rampaged through the streets like an apocalyptic storm. The grown-ups all looked terrified, but their sons were impressed, as were their daughters. Danger seemed to be attractive. It depressed him. Still, he made a thousand birds cry out at once, and scowled at adults from the back of his horse-drawn flatbed. The gun-bearing RedBlacks looked afraid of the boy with the split personality. Their rifles were no match for all those birds.

His father was told that Morgan had fucked up his job. Zvominir screamed at him, bereft, and Morgan screamed back. He said he wouldn't cater to oppressors. It hurt the boy to lie, he really liked de-birding in the suburbs. He said he wanted back in the ghetto. Zvominir said, Out of the question. Morgan threw all kinds of invective about Zvominir's effacement of his limp, how it flattered RedBlacks, etc. But really, he just had to see Katherine.

Please, said his father, don't destroy yourself.

In his birdshow that night, he assembled his creamiest pigeons in the figure of a baby, and placed it in a stroller made of blue jays. Vultures plucked the baby from the carriage, tore it up and ate it in the sky, with cardinals of blood spewing everywhere. Parents were outraged, Zvominir

was terrified—it had unfolded too quick for him
to censor—Jane said she had never been prouder,
she who did not understand.

He had terrified his audience and customers,
so Jane respected him even more. She figured he
had changed on her account, and said as much.
He didn't say he hadn't. They burned buildings at
their leisure, the RedBlacks being numerous but
helpless. No wonder they had lost to the Hungarians; the only kind of war the Judge could win
was on his own people. But Morgan was tired of
waiting for another meeting with Katherine, who
he wanted because she was the daughter of the
Judge, and also because she was hot, and he liked
how it felt when she talked to him, and how he
could not stop thinking about her.

35

The Gypsies who dwelled in the soup kitchen—which actually was a shelter, though, because Morgan called it a soup kitchen, she would call it that, too—died at an incredibly slow speed, their bodies light as bees. Clothes were all that held them to the earth; they were turning into birds. Their eyes had been green, but time and light had bleached them. Katherine helped them raise spoons to their mouths, their hands were so unsteady.

Even if they'd had the strength to use utensils, the food here was ghastly, and Katherine ordered it improved. Her mother would never have set foot in this creaky, blasted home for dying foreigners. Her great grandfather had built it, her grandfather had re-built it, and her father had re-built it again. The kitchen was filthy, the oven was cold, the knives couldn't even spread butter without snapping in two. A table actually collapsed when she put a bowl of soup on it. Katherine told her so-called boss, a bitter woman named Paula, to acquire new appliances. That's impossible, Paula said, we'll never get them, Don't get your hopes up, no one cares what happens here. But Katherine cared. She told her father. He supplied them with utensils that worked, forks with tongs and spoons that didn't leak, tables that could

stand up to a draft when the doors were opened.
Obsolete stoves were likewise replaced. People
who had gone for decades without vegetables ate
peppers that were crisp against their few remaining teeth. So wonderful and strange, fresh food!
The water, which upset her stomach for a week,
would actually be filtered, and the ceiling was replaced, so plaster didn't drizzle on the meals. In
the course of four weeks, Katherine re-invented
the soup kitchen.

   She felt mixed about asking her father for
help, who she was technically still angry at. She
had started to believe that he was capable of
treachery; the awful things she'd heard about
abuse, about the nastiness of RedBlacks, and the
sufferings of the Gypsies, began to seem plausible
to her. Certainly, the misery of the Gypsies was
greater than she'd thought. The notion of working in a soup kitchen struck her on a whim, but
help, she saw, was really needed. When people in
the soup kitchen learned who she was, they stayed
away and didn't talk to her, and she was just as
lonely here as in school, or at home. Everyone was
scared that a Giggs was around, which had to be
her father's fault. But he had been generous with
the kitchen, and the improvements he had funded
changed the lives of many people. He can't be all
that bad, she thought, and began to forgive him.
It was a relief.

   Gypsies flooded to the dining hall. All of them

were hungry, and many were sick; Katherine didn't stop until the kitchen could accommodate them all. She didn't understand the minutia of running a giant kitchen/hospital/social hall/shelter, though Paula did, but Paula had no instincts for improvement, no ambition. Katherine fired her. She interviewed the candidates for Paula's replacement herself, though her father looked on at her request. All of the candidates vomited or wept at the sight of him, so Katherine made him sit behind a screen. Still, she hired the one he liked the best, a skinny man named Kurt who assured her he would never sleep until every Gypsy had been fed.

At her request—a polite word for "command"—Kurt built a tented medical facility in the lots behind the kitchen, for surgery and treatment. Gypsies came from all over the city to be cured there.

Her father had never been more proud of a member of his family, certainly not Mike, nor his wife, ululating in her bedroom. But Mrs. Giggs refused to visit. Stay away from Morgan, she said. This isn't about Morgan, Katherine said, this is really important. She hated how foolish and young her mother made her feel; all of her accomplishments were small in the eyes of this woman. I see why he likes you, she continued, you're quite attractive, but your looks will fade, as mine did.

Whatever, Katherine said. I've beaten you,

and you know it. This was the most decisive thing she could think of to say. She even believed it, partially. She was on a different path then her mother's. Her life would have an impact, and she did what she chose now. She would even go to a birdshow tonight, and sit near the bottom of the Steps, where Morgan would see her.

The monks had helped her mother build an altar at the Giggs house, with incense and images of God. I want to go to The Cloister, said her mother, come with me before you get killed. You know I'm not allowed there, Katherine said, and besides, my life is here. This life is nothing, said her mother, So come with me or don't, I don't suppose it matters in the end. Your fatalism is an act, Katherine said. I don't believe you really think that.

Katherine hired carpenters to erect a stage where Gypsy bands could play. Younger Gypsies came to hear the music, and thronged the space near the stage. She could tell they knew who she was by how they looked at her, peering through the corners of their eyes, afraid to look directly, scared of what the RedBlacks would do to a Gypsy who stared at Katherine Giggs.

36 Morgan used ring-billed gulls for Katherine's face, cardinals for freckles and chiaroscuro hawks, curlews for her hair—their red bending beaks broke the picture-plane, illustrating wind—eyes of green ducks and raven-colored pupils, the shadow of her nose a parallelogram of plovers, nightingales and parakeets for pigment, every bird a spot within a massive field of color-clusters, which all made Katherine Giggs. We know he selected birds for their brilliance, a repertory company of colors. We would like to show you Katherine's face, but we can't see it for ourselves, a madman sought her portraits and destroyed them.

Zvominir arrived a moment late to the Square for the birdshow. He elbowed through the crowd to reach his spot beside the fountain, and saw that Katherine's face had blotted out the sky. Oh fuck, he thought. He tried to blur the portrait, but Morgan, hipped by these distortions to his father's intervention, labored to retain his bird-control, and keep intact his tribute. Katherine herself stared at Morgan from the Steps, amid her RedBlacks, hands clasped beneath her chin. Everyone was looking at her look at him. At first, we thought the Katherine-of-birds was an insult, until we saw her reaction. She looked enchanted.

Morgan's Katherine wasn't critical. It was

rhapsody. Holy shit, we thought. The boy is crazy, he is fearless. He must be in love.

Zvominir bird-distorted furiously, so Morgan tried to hide her face in other illustrations. He transformed images into Katherine: likenesses of streets into Katherine, children into Katherine, rows of marching people into Katherine, thunderclouds, forests and flags into Katherine, white-capped oceans, though he had never seen the sea. Zvominir altered the imagery as soon as he could recognize it, mostly into faces of children whose influential parents he hoped to flatter, and therefore change the evening's emphasis from Morgan doing Katherine—so to speak—to Morgan acting trusty and undangerous.

As Zvominir continued his obstructions, Morgan innuendoed, made of birds men who hid things in jackets, who took off their masks and had no faces. Zvominir admired the completeness of these visions, the meticulous way that his son handled little things: eye color, wrinkles, aluminum siding, carpets, expressions, domestic interiors; the world he created with birds exceeded in detail the world we lived in. The kid was getting better. Nonetheless, Zvominir recognized suggestions of Katherine, her eyes amid clouds and lips in waves, her freckles concealed in a meadow of peonies, veins the currents of rivers. Morgan hadn't planned all the elements of Katherine that Zvominir suppressed; Zvominir saw what he feared to see.

Morgan had been using the birds every day and every night, and practice had made his power equal to his father's. The two were at a stalemate. No one knew that they were fighting, and the show, which had been brilliant until now, devolved into a muddle. We grew bored by this portrayal of what seemed to be a color wheel, or a periodic table; the shock we'd felt at seeing Katherine's face was replaced, in the end, with disappointment. Most of the children decided that Morgan had suffered an off-night, or maybe the performance had been artsy, and they just didn't get it, while adults thought acclaim had burned him out, for they wanted his celebrity to fizzle into failure, and maybe sordid tragedy, a narrative they recognized. We resist original plots. But Katherine didn't care; she was rapt. RedBlacks wouldn't let her talk to him, and shuffled him away toward the ghetto.

37 Katherine never missed another bird-show. The following night, she took her seat near the bottom of the Steps. Everybody else watched the birds, but she watched Morgan, and Jane watched her. Jane had made a special trip to the surface, in disguise as a man, to see if Morgan actually did Katherine's face. She wore a fishing cap and a phony moustache. Morgan hardly used gestures at all, and controlled the birds with his expressions, while Zvominir muttered by the fountains. RedBlacks with guns were posted in the Square and on the Steps, and did their best to look unawed. It didn't work. They were terrified. Everybody was.

Jane saw what they said she'd see: hints of Katherine in the patterns on the sky, disappearing at the moment she would recognize them. It was true. She was furious, if not exactly shocked, that Morgan was preoccupied with Katherine, but she also saw, to some extent, what Morgan saw in her. Katherine was downy, freshly cute and innocent, and seemed bereft of pathos, although, as the daughter of the Judge, there must certainly be some darkness there, even if strangers couldn't find it. More than hate, Jane felt pity. Here was the oblivious and well-meaning child of a monumental sociopath whose crimes would tar her name forever and bring ruin to a family and a city and two peoples, an epic shitstorm brewing just around the corner that would destroy her, and the girl had no idea, she was taking in a birdshow and flirting with the boy whose magic gift would guarantee her doom. Adorable! On another day, Jane would have admitted that Katherine was hot, in a kiss-me-under-the-bleachers kind of way, but this was not that day, and she really needed Katherine to fuck off before her powers of distraction turned Morgan's head for good.

We assumed that Katherine did more than see his birdshows. We figured she snuck out of the kitchen to join in the parade of his debirding. Since he'd been returned to his bird-route in the ghetto, his debirding had become a *Carnivale* of Gypsies who tagged along around his horse-drawn flatbed, crying out their prayers to the birds. None of these Gypsies worked, though where would they work? There weren't any jobs, which of course was not our fault, we didn't ask them to come here. It seemed as though they'd thronged our city just to join the Swede boy in the streets, hooting and dancing, though supposedly they starved, and so many of their bones had been smashed by RedBlacks or the cops of other cities they had lived in; the yellowy complexions they owed to malnutrition, their bulging eyeballs redolent of bird-inflected manias, and they never seemed to eat, and sang and danced their days away, skulking on corners, anger glar-ing through their eyes. We even heard they beat themselves in frenzied exaltation, thrashing their bodies with sacks of stones and onions, writhing on the muddy city streets among the vermin and cats who feasted on the birds, and were feasted on by birds. Morgan and his flatbed headed the parade. Behind him were the altars, the effigies, the birdfloats made of feathers and the children dressed as birds, nostalgic for death—we didn't blame them—and then there were the penitent, those who thrashed their bodies that the birds within their flesh would not degrade, the soul is trapped and horrified within its fleshy prison, for flesh contains desire, but feathers don't. Every-where, from front to back, the minstrels played their music, and always in time with each other.

We heard that Katherine joined the parades, disguised in a wig and patchwork clothes, mes-merized by birds that Morgan hoarded overhead, to flout us with in birdshows. We were certain, certain she was with him. All of us had whispered it.

38 The tutor heard rumors of Morgan and Katherine, watched his fellow Red-Blacks laugh and joke at her expense in unmentionable ways—she probably gets bird-fucked, they said—until officers ordered them to stop, but the soldiers still whispered it, to tease him. After doing Katherine's portrait twice, Morgan had been ordered not do it again, ever. And he'd agreed. Days of obedience had passed. The Bird Boy, thought the tutor, must be sating his desire in other ways.

The tutor had given Katherine his poems. He'd written them for her. She didn't care. He'd courted her earnestly and slowly, to no effect at all. She hadn't even trifled with him. He found himself alone in the military bathroom, searching the puzzle of his face, his olive-shaped head and chubby features that belied his brittle frame. He considered his fate, who did not believe in fate until this moment. His fate was to be lonely and sad, a servant for an over-privileged moron, and the customer of whores.

He smashed the mirror with his pistol-butt, and hoped that someone would step on the shards.

He rode into the city to spy on Katherine, and cased the building where she had her little kitchen, the vanity project endowed by her father, his employer, who'd condemned him to despair. Or had he condemned himself?He saw that the facility wasn't small, but gigantic, and uselessly monumental—like all things built by a Giggs. It was even clean and fragrant. He heard she'd fixed the place up, but what he saw defied his expectations. Gone was the crumbling plaster and the fallen rafter heaps: the roof had been enforced with steel girders. The floors had been mopped into squint-inducing brightness, and didn't smell of garbage. All the dirty broken windows had been replaced. The space was filled with misty light, like a smoke of blood and shadow. Aged, sickly Gypsies doddered everywhere, but didn't look unhappy. This was probably the first pleasant place they'd seen in memory; it certainly exceeded the pleasures of the military mess hall. There was even a band. If you had to decay, this would be the place to do it. The improvements had all been made by Katherine. She had actually accomplished something here; more than something. This was no vanity project.

He taught evil for money.

He poked around the kitchen and the offices, roamed the ratless alleys she must've had cleaned, and swept through the kitchen again, and the medical pavilion. People he asked said she left after dinner, in the hour or so before the birdshow.

She was probably with Morgan. He plotted

out the schedule of her day—school, soup kitchen, bird-parade, dinner, free time, birdshow, back to her house—which confirmed what he already felt. The facts could only match his intuition. She and that little Swede were somewhere in the city, probably nearby. The kitchen wasn't far from the Steps; Morgan could meet with her in secret for a time before his birdshow, and nobody would notice.

The hole into the underground the tutor had used to search out Morgan and his father had since been sealed with concrete by the rebels of the tunnels. Tortured Gypsies had disclosed the operation, and soldiers had been sent to check their truth-claims. This worthless datum, by the way, was the only useful information gleaned from torture that the tutor could recall. He left the kitchen and the green zone that surrounded it, and waded through the streets full of carriages and horses, pushing through dangerous-looking Gypsies. He didn't feel particularly safe here. Everything looked threatening in the city. The buildings were tall and overpopulated, tenements built by whom, owned by whom, unmaintained and unpoliced. Criminals or rebels could be anywhere, and probably were everywhere. People hung laundry on lines strung across the city canyons; clothes overhead like tattered banners, rippling in ragged undefeat. How could these people be subjected and brought into line, not that they were guilty,

they were innocent, but their innocence insinu-
ated. They'd love to see the likes of him get killed.
The tutor knew that tunnels mazed beneath the
streets; they were almost totally unmapped. Red-
Blacks ceded sewers to the Gypsies by default, so
dank and fetid, and only lit by nightplants, weeds
impossible and foul. There must be an entrance
here somewhere. Most of the street level businesses were bars and shot-up storefronts, bo-
degas and pawn shops, with shelves of old food,
rusty guns and switchblades and old model ships
trapped in bottles.

The tutor wandered into a saloon that looked
especially swampy, the kind of bar whose blackness seemed forever pure of sunlight, where the
pallid hands of drunks shook like creatures born
too soon, and radiated light, the only light. He
bumped through blackness, waiting for his eyes
to adjust. Cigarette smoke white as alabaster
wrenched, like something trying to free itself from
chains. He sat on a stool at the bar, a crumbled
edifice of stickiness, and ordered a shot of bour-
bon and a beer.

The bartender smiled. The tutor couldn't tell
if he was mocking him, or actually friendly. People had a way of smiling which insulted. He figured that the bartender knew he was important,
and maybe recognized him, though he wasn't in
his uniform; this was undercover work. He wore
his dangerous leather jacket, his pistol in a hol-

ster at his waist. His drinks arrived. He drank the shot and felt it stab its way down. Another shot, he said.

He downed the second shot, took the mug and drifted toward the bathroom, the smoke-marbled darkness getting darker. He entered the long and narrow bathroom, with urinals, a stall, and yellow-brown mirror he didn't want to use, he hated what he looked like. The scene was about what he'd expected, right down to the light bulb that dangled from the ceiling like the head-lamp of a deep-sea fish. He set down his mug on a urinal. An old man came out from the stall, and struggled with his zipper. Probably his hands no longer worked; he probably had arthritis. Good thing I'm still young, thought the tutor.

The man seized the tutor's neck, and another man—a second man appeared from the stall, and then a third—pulled his gun from the holster. The second man hit him on the head with the gun. He felt himself collapse.

39 They took his money, and his gun, and his clothes. He woke up on the street, in an alley, where the rats from the kitchen appeared to have relocated. They clustered near a dumpster, in a heap, a frantic pile of roiling fur. The tutor tried to stand.

The wound on his head still bled, and he wore a Gypsy's clothes: an old suit coat, no shirt, pants too big, held up by a handkerchief tied between the two front loops. His feet were bare, his wallet gone. They had dressed him up as them. He fell back to the ground amid the bits of glass and garbage. It took a day to find his way back to his barracks. RedBlacks mistook him for a Gypsy, and harassed him for pleasure. They could not believe he was the tutor, and yet when he explained what had happened, they believed him. Only you, they said. In the barracks, the guards had some laughs at his expense when they saw him so disheveled. He approached the shattered mirror. His face was untouched.

He rode to the Judge's estate, and found Mike in the yard, running with his band, and Tom and Gus.

Punch me, said the tutor. Beat my face into a mess. Are you crazy, Mike asked, I won't do it. Tom and Gus said, We'll do it! You guys back off, said the tutor. It's between me and him. I don't want to hit you, Mike said. You're a pussy, said the tutor. A coward, a girl, a fag, afraid to fight.

As the tutor hurled insults, Mike hit him, blasting punches at his face, swung his hands like hammers.

40 Nightplants throbbed along the walls of the tunnels, like arteries of light. Morgan liked to walk here, in the silence or the echoing of banging Gypsy music. He could hear the songs and saw the silhouettes of Gypsies whose faces he might recognize in daylight. Jane set the pace up ahead. Supposedly, she knew where they were going, though she seemed to be lost. They had doubled back so many times, paused at corners, wandered and meandered, that he had almost said they'd be late for their meeting. She toyed with him, he felt, as a hunter does with easy prey. She stopped again, looked up and down the tunnel. What now, he said.

She turned, looked right into his face, and took a very deep breath. He'd never seen her look afraid before.

Everyone says you're fucking her.

Who, he said.

I'm going to say this as calmly as I can, Jane said. If you're seeing Katherine Giggs behind my back, you have to either tell me, or stop immediately. We're in too deep for you to screw things up. This isn't just about you, it's about the Gypsies, and the future of this city. Thousands and thousands of lives are at stake, including hers, and I don't know if you've considered this, but she is almost certainly going to be killed by people who worship you, people you empower every day, so if you give a fuck about this girl, you have to be coherent.

Birds which had followed them had leaped onto Jane, and she swiped them away.

I don't know where you got this idea, he said, but it isn't true.

Be honest, she said. You won't get another chance.

I'm innocent, he said.

Swear on the ghost of your mother, she said.

I swear, he said.

Forgive me, mom, he thought. I'm fucking Katherine Giggs. How can I admit it to Jane?

Jane said, I'm pregnant.

41

He was not prepared to be a father. He didn't make enough money, and the money he did have he didn't want to spend on a child. He was cheating on Jane every day, and couldn't stop if he wanted to, which he didn't.

Morgan and Jane met the arsonists later that night, in an underground bar, one of many which had opened in the tunnels, along with restaurants and stores. This might be the ugliest bar I've ever seen, Morgan thought; the ceiling was so low that even he, who was not exactly tall, had to duck. It was more like a crawl space. Birthday candles gave the only light, the bar dark as a moonless sky of stars. The darkness didn't stop Gypsies from thrashing out their *ska* from what looked like a pit. The roof and floor were stone, the walls lined with flimsy wood panels that looked like they'd been stacked there. No one seemed upset by the conditions but Morgan; everybody drank and laughed like happy people. Poverty embarrassed him. He knew he should act like he enjoyed dumps like this; he knew that indifference to luxury was morally superior, that avarice was rotten. He wished the band would stop their jolly clamor, which oppressed him, for music couldn't touch him in this filth, and reminded him he couldn't think nice thoughts on command. All these normal, well-adjusted, gladly poor and music-loving people were a torment. He thought of the bars Mike Giggs probably went to, the fancy decorations and furnishings he couldn't imagine. Mike Giggs frolicked in lavish surroundings while his kind were trapped beneath the Earth. Poverty degrades you, he thought, and worrying about it makes you petty.

He didn't feel prepared to be a father.

Jane led him deep into the mildew-smelling cavern, where they sat at a candlelit table with Ezekiel and Jim, who were among the hundred rebel arsonists inspired by Morgan, and to some extent Jane, who they felt dubious about, though she did have clever plans that never failed, and when they burned without her sanction, they often got pinched and disappeared, or caught on fire themselves. She may not have rallied them, but they looked to her to organize them.

Morgan couldn't tell the two apart, all Gypsies looked alike, though these two seemed unusually tall, and not as messy as expected, and stronger, their biceps busting from their shirts. He thought of Katherine's shoulders, a place he liked to bite. He had tried to crush her in his arms, but she was stronger than she looked—a chick with muscles; she said she could do chin-ups—and almost crushed him. If only she had crushed him. After, he'd apologized for having been brutal, but Katherine told him not to. It wasn't that he loved her, he wanted to ride out to the middle of the venus flytrap river and get eaten for her. Her love for him improved his own opinion of himself, at least when she was there. Otherwise, he was a liar, an adulterer, a leader who would surely be unmasked as a fraud, and a soon-to-be deadbeat dad. Could he maybe take a mulligan on being the messiah?

He made up his mind not to think about Katherine, Jane might see it on his face. Ezekiel and Jim cracked their knuckles. If they wanted to attack him, he'd have no way to defend himself, unless he used the knife at his ankle, though Ezekiel and Jim looked strong enough to easily disarm him. Could underfed people get this big? It didn't seem likely. They looked like bouncers. He knew he shouldn't think this, but Jim's cock must be huge. He wanted to clutch at Katherine, he had never clutched at anyone, he had always been too proud.

He was thinking about Katherine again.

Ezekiel and Jim said it was incredible to meet him, they were humbled, they had never missed a birdshow, and were ready to do anything he asked. Others had wanted to meet him too, and would come another time, there were fires to be set, they hoped he understood. Sitting on a milk crate—no chairs in this bar—he knew he should be listening to Ezekiel, but he couldn't do that either. He couldn't do anything. His father had predicted that Jane would get pregnant. Right as usual. How would Katherine take the news? He felt, not like a man, but an empty house of voices that screamed across each other in rages.

He still hadn't spoken. I told you he was quiet, said Jane, and shared a smile with the others. They said there were hundreds of youths who would fight against the RedBlacks. They were tired of being punching bags. Don't call us Gypsies anymore, said Ezekiel, we're from Norway, we're Norwegians, and this will be our land. The band came to the end of their song, and the audience leaped, enthralled, and banged their heads on the ceiling. Can we get you a drink, asked Jim, rubbing his head. I don't drink, Morgan said. It was more-or-less a lie. At least you talk, Jim said. Not unless I have to say no, Morgan said. We know you don't take shit from anyone, said Ezekiel.

Ezekiel and Jim turned out to be brothers, and the sons of professors. Their family had lived in the city for many generations, and weren't poor at all. In fact, they had grown up in the suburbs, and Morgan even knew their house. It was bloody huge. They probably went to school with Mike Giggs, back when Mike still went to school. Did they know Katherine? He decided not to ask.

Ezekiel didn't drink either, and he prayed, not to gods, but to ideals, to a godless void of pure human justice and potential, to a perfect empty heaven. Think of a godhead without god, he explained. No personality, formless and pure, though of course it had a gender: it was male. Jim coughed into his hand and said *Bullshit*!

Jim didn't share his brother's faith. Jim loved fire, and rebellion for its own sake. He liked a good time. Ezekiel thought the god-without-god gave Norwegians a template for ruling the city, though Jim seemed ambivalent to the notion of real responsibility. Ezekiel used words like theocracy, strict, and tradition; Jim said things like party, dude, booze, and cookies. They made Jane and Morgan miss Billy.

The only thing I care about is birds, Morgan said, I'm a patriot to nothing but the sky. Jane scowled. This generic prophet bullshit is what came out of his mouth when he couldn't figure out what to say, and Jane knew it, though she was courteous enough to not embarrass him. Her policy was never make a teammate look like shit in public. Of course we'll take care of the birds, Ezekiel said. We love them, they are us; they are how we know it's time to make our home here, they're a sign, and so are you. Morgan thought, I don't feel like a sign.

The band's set ended, and they climbed out from their hole. Jane said it was time to set some fires. Morgan silently accompanied them through tunnels that throbbed with secret plants. He helped to burn a law firm, where a neighbor of Ezekiel and Jim worked. These two are dangerous, Morgan thought. They blow up neighbors' businesses. What would they do if they discovered his relationship with Katherine? He emptied some desks, littering the office with papers and setting them afire, watching as flames spent their rages in the dark, as though there could be no transcendence, just oblivion or fury.

They stood on a rooftop while the office burned across the street. Jane told Ezekiel and Jim that she and Morgan would be married, which he'd agreed to in the time between their little conference and the meeting in the bar. They were going to have a baby, she continued.

The Bird Boy thought back to his swans, to his beloved little baby Heathcliff, the only other child he'd ever cared for, and look how that turned out. Morgan had sworn to get revenge, but there could be no vengeance on the people who deserved it. He would either share in senseless acts of violence, or else be pulled apart, like Heathcliff had been.

42

The tutor, bruised and ugly, could go unseen now in the city, in his shredded Gypsy clothes. He returned to the bar where he'd been mugged; no one recognized him there. Three men had come out from the stall in the bathroom, so he went for that stall. The toilet swiveled on a hinge, and beneath it was a hole. Elementary copcraft: check behind all doors. He lowered himself into the tunnel, where night-plants fringed the tunnel dark like moonlight, a frostiness that made him think of childhood, back when there was hope. What did he hope for now? To find her with the Swede?

Don't be so dramatic, he thought. You're supposed to be a soldier.

He took out his compass and headed for the soup kitchen. The tunnels weren't straight, which didn't surprise him, but the quality of curvature surprised him. They seemed more like accidental space-irruptions, and possessed the random excellence of tree roots, the perfectly inscrutable shape of nature, which is never comprehensible or ugly. Light here lacked the yellow lemonness of sunlight; a pallor as of corpses lit the tunnel. And yet, it would be wrong to say that no life flourished; it seemed that twice as many people roamed here, compared to the surface.

He rivered through eddies of Gypsies, goats, sheep, pushcarts and bassoons. How could this place smell of food, when supposedly the Gypsies had no food? He counted his steps until he reached what he guessed was the space beneath the soup kitchen, where the search for Katherine's hideout could begin. He stood in an arena with an altar at one end, like a huge place of worship, whether people sang their *ska* prayers at the birds who'd made their nests on the roof, and crammed it thick with sticks. If there'd been a floorplan for the tunnels, he could hardly conceive it. No wonder the Swede and Katherine couldn't be caught among these many-chambered curves, this network he could never find the end of; no wonder Hungary had failed to take the city, when they'd occupied the surface.

He'd taken an oath to find Katherine before he had known what the oath entailed. But the oath remained. He started by counting the ventricles feeding this he-called-it-an-arena, of which there were twelve, or thirteen, or maybe fourteen, it was hard to distinguish. Each had its own set of curves and digressions, some offered nothing but darkness. He would have to scrutinize each route, make replicas in his mind.

Teenage boys with slatterns on their arms stood at the bend of every tunnel, pistols in their belts. They seemed to be chewing on the scenery, while younger children carried messages. This

must be their turf. They were probably connected to the arsonists. He had grudgingly marveled
at their acumen and courage, their excellence at
warcraft. They could burn the building of their
choice, and RedBlacks couldn't stop them. Mike
and I should torture us some kids, thought the tutor, and see where that gets us. Even if it doesn't
get us anywhere, at least we'll have tortured us
some kids. He used to think that torture was
barbaric, but now it didn't seem to bother him.
Funny, that.

The Judge conducted torture in the basement
of his mansion's coach house, a chamber called
The BoomBoom Room. Torture seemed like comfort food to him. He had either loved causing pain
all his life, or experience had transformed him.
The tutor knew how that could happen; it was
happening to him.

He started with the tunnels underneath the
soup kitchen, walking up and down the walls, to
look for any curtains, false doors, or to listen for
her voice. He found bupkis, except for doddering
old folks. Only a fool would have their tryst this
close to their job, and Katherine was no fool.

The next tunnel dealt in books. He searched
through the bookshelves and piles of stolen vol-
umes, most of which he'd hardly ever heard of,
and he spent too much time reading poems in the
light of dark-fed plants, and stocked up on the
Yoknapatawpha novels, and the LA Quartet. Now

he looked even more incognito: he carried books! In addition, he pretended to be crazy and impaired, and it wasn't really that much of a stretch, he could only fully see with his left eye. Nobody would think he had a gun, let alone three guns beneath his trenchcoat.

Past the bookshelves were livestock that languished in lagoons, wading in puddles of their excrement, mostly sheep and hogs, and smaller pigs. The tutor pitied them. He hadn't eaten meat since he was nine, and the thought of killing made him sick. Katherine didn't eat meat, either. He scratched the doomed head of a goat, and scrutinized the place for secret hideouts, or tried to, but even nightplants flickered in the horrible aroma, and he could find nothing. In this tunnel, Gypsies slept in puddles and sold garbage to each other, turned ruined packaging into furniture, reposed in wrappers, wore cartons as their clothes.

We see no reason to enlarge upon the vomiting spells, angry departures, grudging and desperate returns of the tutor. He failed to sleep in his creaky metal bunk, the bed of an inmate. Sleep can be accomplished if the sleeper is thoroughly relaxed, his body at rest, his mind gone blank. He had eaten food from the tunnels in order to assimilate, and now his stomach suffered, and he scrambled to and from his little bathroom. There seemed to be a part of him that craved its own turmoil. His mind: a labyrinth of secrets and darkness, where thoughts could roam and scheme, unpoliced. He swore to defenestrate the wilds of his soul, to clear-cut his mind and drive his seeming inner vulnerable self toward the light. Where he'd kill it.

He took the Yoknapatawpha books back to the tunnel, and tossed them on a bonfire. He kept the Ellroy. Fuck doubt. The universe can be conquered. Before, he'd seen the tunnels as Death's antechamber, a grim bazaar of solemn scarred survivors, their minds in other rooms, other times, which they helplessly remembered. Now he saw them all as enemies of state and suckers waiting to be exploited. Many of them babbled, or leaned against the walls, staring blackly into nothing. Emotions were actual things with physical consequences. He could use that against them.

His face had started healing; he would have to be re-beaten.

The tunnels had weapons for sale: switchblades, bayonets, pistols and rifles, all rusted, most of them obsolete and many of them vintage; he could start a business dealing weapons to wealthy collectors, who loved old guns. Gypsies, he learned, had restored the original name of their tribe, and were now called *Norwegians*. Norway, neighbor to Sweden. How had Norwegians come as far as this city? He smashed his face with a concrete lump, in everybody's view. No one looked surprised as he bled; no one looked at all.

Mourners flooded the underground arena, and their cries stabbed his ears. Coffins were passed overhead, bobbing like corpses on water, and banners that portrayed the Judge's face were set on fire. This must be a remnant of Morgan's bird-parade, an after-party party for fanatics, of which it looked like there were hundreds. The departed must be rebels that the army had killed. At the rate Norwegians died in confrontations with the RedBlacks, funeral insurrection scenes must happen every day down here, a constant rage convulsion that grew on what it made. The tutor, freshly bloodied from his self-inflicted wounds, joined the train, arousing no suspicion; so many others bled as well, and what was his bloody face compared to theirs, but a thing they had in common? The crowd lunged in vociferating currents. This would be when Katherine and the Swede would be together, when nobody was looking.

Throngs spread in every direction, up and down the tunnels and impossible to follow or examine, except anecdotally. He watched as the crowd broke into little mourning clusters, which seemed oddly jovial and boisterous, what with how supposedly they grieved. The birdshow was nigh. He emerged with his group through the brown and dumpy employee lounge of a five-and-dime store, which sold mostly party decorations.

Norwegians were kept on the far side of the Square, opposite the Steps, where their view of birds was limited. He joined the Norwegians who lied on their backs in the street, rivers of them flooding through the city. Above, a sky of birds stretched their wings in preparation for the show. RedBlacks enforced the separation of natives and Norwegians. The Bird Boy made his birds appear as RedBlacks, and RedBlacks transformed into trees swarmed by refugees of Norway. The birds, trees and refugees he whirled into clouds that churned into babies, a sky full of babies, all alike. It was sentimental. Usually the images were hostile to RedBlacks, or at least incomprehensible, but this seemed downright sweet. What was he trying to do, kiss and make up?

Image after image of unity, and children who laughed. Was there one laughing child in the whole fucking city, with the birds and the fires and the post-traumatic stress disorders suffered by the parents of the children? What kind of artist was he? Was this the dangerous rogue Katherine loved? After the show, the tutor waded through Norwegians toward the Steps, and saw that Morgan kicked a soccer ball with his father. Weren't they supposed to hate each other's guts? Had they reached some kind of truce, or were reports of their disputes oversimplified? Why was everyone so happy? Katherine stood with some brand-new friends from the soup kitchen. Her face deployed expressions he had never seen, smiles of joy and mischief, evidence of a thousand inside jokes. He hardly recognized this strange familiar person, and even when she looked right at his face—which happened twice, chilling him both times—she didn't recognize him. Her secret liaisons with Morgan had done wonders for her looks, while he had been disfigured. He'd given himself to Katherine, but she had passed him over. His poems had been read unremarked, or tossed away like junk mail.

There was nothing left to do but destroy her.

43

But he couldn't find the place where she and Morgan had their lair, their *fuckpad*, as the LA Quartet called it.

He found himself alone beside an aquifer gone black with pollution, a still sea of tar, which lay behind a barrier of spiderwebs, a wilderness of silk. He tossed a chunk of stone into the pool, and it was ploplessly absorbed. He had seen tunnels with doctors, lawyers, hookers, stolen furniture and Renaissance re-enactments, and weapons, endless rows of weapons, but had failed to departmentalize them. Regions of the tunnel did not have specific demarcations, but flowed like seas into the sea, impossible to map. Maps were imaginary constructs, but they were also power, for they conquered the world. He would make a fucking map. He returned to the arena, and stood near the cluster of elderly Gypsies. Behind them, at their feet, was the entrance to a passageway he hadn't seen before, an opening slightly larger than a varmint-hole, though the tunnel it fed was big enough to accommodate countless senile people. He crawled inside the hole, where ancient Norwegians blindly gazed at the white light of nightplants. Did they know where they were? He didn't like to generalize, but this he knew for certain: no one in the geriatric tunnel seemed to recognize their plight; their faces were blank.

44

No recognition, he thought. They could not say what they knew, or what they'd seen.

They were here, he knew it, they had to be here. Yes, this tunnel lay beneath the soup kitchen, a place he'd already ruled out. Perhaps he'd been too hasty. Be a detective! He kicked old Gypsies out of his way, and they groaned, and he liked it. They smelled like piss, he didn't care about the smell. Katherine and the Bird Boy must be here. Nobody could turn them in here, and Katherine loved old people. She felt comfortable around them. Girls always talked about feeling safe; *I feel safe with him*, they said, and only about boys who were anything but safe.

He bowled over elderly Gypsies to get to the tunnel wall, which he scrutinized for approximately a mile, until the tunnel did its tunnel thing and altered its identity, all of the sudden there were tanks of nitrous oxide, and children who sucked them. Junkies. Fuck them. He would come back for their lives. He worked his way back on the tunnel's other side. He was going to catch them. Methodical patterns of searching yielded nothing, but circles had worked. He was truly a poet; his mused prized indirection. His muse he would kidnap, torture and brainwash to his cause, until it got with the program. There could be no doubt that it felt lovely to destroy, better than it felt to create. This is why the world could not improve. He had passed the point of giving a shit.

Halfway down the tunnel, he came upon three chickadees.

He got on his knees and scrutinized the floor, until he found a heap of wet rags, which he nudged to the side to find a metal sewer grate. What kind of urban planner puts a sewer grate at the bottom of a sewer? He squinted to see through the bars. Bodies, side, by side, and a blanket. Toucans on the floor.

Katherine and Morgan.

45 Morgan had begun to fear the surface. Norwegians were an inch away from rioting, many carried weapons, staves and clubs and bats they'd spiked with nails, not to mention guns, and he knew how the RedBlacks would react to any challenge. He feared what Jane would do to Katherine when she discovered proof of the affair. He found himself afraid to disappoint his father, and marveled at the way the man had gone about his business, had somehow stayed unkilled these many years. How had he done it?

Morgan spent whatever time he could with Katherine in the underground apartment, which she'd found while looking at schematics of the soup kitchen. The apartment had a shower, a daybed, an icebox, and a small sewer grate in the ceiling; she'd crammed it with rags. Morgan and Katherine lay on the daybed, beneath a checkered tablecloth. He bathed her in the shower and cooked for her, and wanted to do more, do domestic things, pretend to be the man he'd never be, but mostly it was she who cared for him, by giving him her body.

I wish you'd untie that knife on your leg, she would say. I swore an oath, he'd answer, to my swans, though speaking these words seemed pointless now, his vows unsaid themselves with saying.

Norwegians worshipped the dawn re-arrival of the birds, which blocked the horizon and the sunrise, sunlight blazing through fissures in the flocks. But Morgan begged the birds to stay away. They could all get killed, too. Surely the RedBlacks would attempt to crush the Norway insurrection; Jane had her response all planned—she would never stop attacking, would parry and return with all her strength—and Morgan was expected to participate, to help the revolution. People he knew would be killed. His father would try to protect him, which he would make impossible, for that was his gift: to ruin his father's hope.

One morning, as the two prepared for work, he asked his father to collaborate with him on a birdshow.

Huh?

I want you on stage with me, said Morgan. It'll be fun.

The Bird Man had been polishing his shoes at the dinner table while Morgan rinsed dishes in the basin. Zvominir looked up from his shoes and said he hadn't done a bird performance since he was a child. Actually, said Morgan, you do them every night, only no one knows but me. I don't know how it would look if I got involved, Zvominir said. It would look like we were happy, said Morgan. People might calm down.

That night, they built trees of birds they

limned in red, massive heads with wreaths of wrens, parrot-toucan-peacock rainbows, they even put on plays, in which the brown birds—sparrows; owls—made a stage, while ostriches and herons were the actors, with a crowd of egrets that sat among the real crowd of humans. Partridges zoomed at the stage, at Zvominir's command. It turned out he liked chaos. He also made a cormorant kick-line, and a globe of the moon.

Jane had begun to plan the wedding, and Morgan would be a father, have a child of his own to protect. He could not protect himself, and Jane was not exactly engaged in safe pursuits. The child seemed doomed.

He couldn't tell Katherine of the fires he had set, for she might tell her father—or, worse, her brother—and he needed her approval. In truth, he barely spoke to her at all, to keep from saying things he might regret.

More Norwegian kids joined the rebels every day. The arsons allured like something bigger than a trend: a cause, a calling from above, with Morgan as the messenger, and Jane as the crew chief, who drew up all the schedules and made everybody work more than they wanted, and dealt with terrestrial facts that seemed annoying, but which had to get done, as opposed to the Bird Boy, whose realm was silent magic.

She put the rebel number at a thousand.

The strongest recruitment tool Jane had,

even stronger than Morgan, was the RedBlacks themselves. They enjoyed the tacit and unerring support of their constituents to kill, beat, maim, exploit and torture Norwegians. Newspapers didn't even need to be suppressed: they censored themselves. Norway was used to abuse; inured, in fact, by many generations of exile. But RedBlacks were as bad as anything they'd suffered in Angola, Oklahoma or China. The Judge stoked the flames he meant to smother with his tactics of brutality: his cure was the disease. Looking at the city in flames, Jane wondered how people this dumb could've built a city in the first place.

During the parades, which Morgan dreaded, he had started shunting the birds to the forests in a bland and hurried manner, to defuse the angry crowd. He actually pitied the unsuspecting Red-Blacks, for so many would be killed. He'd started to think that some of them were pretty decent guys. Of course, they were awful, and committed dreadful acts, but once you got to know them, they didn't seem all that bad. In his birdshows, he purged any subtext of anger. He saw that it was easier to act on rage than it was to act on patience. His father grimly shook his head at him, while Jane planned for war. Katherine had always been satisfied with him, for she didn't really know him. After the performance, wealthy children in pricey simulacra of Norway's fashions asked for his autograph. He gave it, and tried to smile politely at their parents, as if to sell the notion that Gypsies were nice, and misunderstood. Perhaps if everybody liked him, they'd spaz the hell down.

He started begging Jane to stop the arson, with the usual success he found whenever he attempted to persuade her. Nobody would listen unless he told them what they already believed. Katherine felt present to him always, and he wanted to impress her, to explain all the things he had done, and repent of his transgressions, live a normal, little life. He wanted to be seen as a birdkeeper, a public health official whose field of expertise was birds. He wanted to be different. He thought, Dad, I want you to be proud of me.

46 To be involved with Morgan was a terrifying burden. Katherine couldn't carry it alone.

She couldn't tell her father, who would probably murder Morgan himself, and also Zvominir, and many Gypsies, too. The handful of Gypsies who'd dared to befriend her in the soup kitchen disappeared for days, re-appearing scared to meet her eyes, their bruises plain to see, and none of them could walk without a stagger, and some had gone blind. She knew where they'd been, and what had happened to them. Her father had no call to do this, they couldn't all be arsonists; he did it just to spite her. She went to his office in the city, burst into a meeting and ordered him to stop, in full view of his officers. She said that she would not be implicated by his methods; enforcing the law was one thing; disgracing her, and her endeavor, to be so cowardly about it, so passive-aggressive, was another. I'm your child, she said. What is wrong with you?

The officers trampled each other in a stampede for the door, afraid to know that someone dared to contradict the boss. The Judge started weeping. You're my hero, he said, and took her in his arms. Katherine herself was overcome with emotion, especially when he promised not to troll for rebels in her kitchen anymore, and, indeed, Gypsies stopped disappearing. She was happy until she realized he would find his innocents elsewhere. Her father had played her. He endowed her project just to get her to shut up, to demonstrate his ownership of her.

She couldn't trust her mother, who knew she'd taken up with Morgan on the very day it happened. She took one look at her daughter, shook her head and said, I told you not to do it. Katherine didn't even try denying it; she crept off to her room and gently closed the door. How could she be so transparent to her mother? It was just a lucky guess, she tried to think, something spoken to antagonize, speculative nonsense, forgotten the instant it was said. Her mother knew from sheer intuition, but had no right to know. She went to see her mother at dawn, in her bedroom, the Judge asleep in his office downstairs.

Katherine begged her mother not to tell the Judge. Her mother said she never told him anything.

Morgan was impetuous, at first. He had crawled through a hole in the floor of the soup kitchen office, locked the door and kissed her, his skin still marked by bruises. To be desired by this god was overwhelming; she had prayed for this moment. His legs were skinnier than hers, and he looked so desperate and unhealthy. She made a point of feeding him and washing him. To have

this kind of access was obscene, a fantasy come
true.

She wanted to consume him in her body. They met in the room below the kitchen every day, between the parade and the birdshow. He hardly spoke at all, and when he did, it was to say that there were things he shouldn't say. The violence was coming, he warned, and she should leave before it hit, he was scared for her life, he endangered her. She said she wasn't scared. It was a lie.

But the boldness he had shown was really bluster. He was scared, and either paced the little room, or took her on the bed. At first, she'd liked the anonymity of their love, the way he needed her body, if not quite her personality, which he appeared to hardly notice, but sex, she finally decided, should not be so aloof, so purely physical and distant from the minds of the people who were having it. If she was to be in love, she needed to be more than just a body to her lover. Don't you want to know me, she asked, I want to know you.

He wouldn't answer.

She had treated enough sick Gypsies to know when she was acting like a nurse. He prowled back and forth like a madman or clenched at her body. He said he didn't want to be responsible. Responsible for what, she asked. He wouldn't say. She said he could either talk or leave, she didn't like the terms of their relationship.

He left.

His birdshows got bleak and unwatchable. Colors sludged into colors, like a mudslide of paint. The audience booed, and Katherine felt responsible. She could barely see him in the shadows at the bottom of the Steps; the dark had had its way with him. He came to her office again, and begged to be taken back. What was she supposed to do?

Once she took him back, the birdshows transcended their old greatness. She saw that he required her in order to continue with his bird-art, which is what she'd always wanted, but having what she wanted brought no happiness.

She figured Morgan had some contact with the arsonists, but never said a word to anyone. Her mother also never spoke. They both could keep a secret.

But the burden of a double life was horrible. Katherine couldn't sleep and lost her appetite; she wasn't made for lying. She needed to tell somebody, but who? She finally had friends in the soup kitchen, but how could she confess her affair to them, who might be tortured by her father? Her father could find out she'd been with Morgan, kill Morgan and Zvominir, shut the soup kitchen. Her brother could find out, and who knew what the hell he'd do. Her mother could reveal her; someone could see Morgan in the kitchen, or see it in her face. She could get unlucky, or Morgan could. The Gypsies could get angry and organize, which everyone she knew in the suburbs waited for with dread, or the RedBlacks could forcibly repatriate the Gypsies to the border. The birds could all die, or drown the city. Her mother could say that she had told her so. Lying was a crime, and once a crime starts, it never stops.

47 The Judge watched his wife leave the house in the company of sackcloth-clad monks, and Zvominir watched the Judge from the lawn. The day before, Mrs. Giggs had been pulled by the gardeners from the stickheap of her rosebush, which she'd torn from the earth, and now her hands and arms were thornbloodied.

Mrs. Giggs had tried to take her children with her to the Cloister, tried to drag them from their rooms, screaming they would die, they would die, he would kill them, they would die as Charlie died. RedBlacks finally pried her off her children, whose arms were scarred from all her clinging. Zvominir had watched the Judge all morning, watched him roam the yards and gaze at his reflection in the pools, check his watch, poke at bushes with a stick. He never went inside to say goodbye to his wife.

The parrots had refused to be dislodged from the estate, they had brought their parrot families, parrot friends, and entire parrot cities, and spoke things said in confidence, as when, for example, the Judge had questioned the veracity of Mike's soaring test scores, which the parrots promptly blabbed. Mike had heard the parrots parrot his father's disbelief; had shot at them, missed, left

a shattered chandelier, and retreated to his room
to play his clarinet, which wept on his behalf, every note a sweet-natured sob of awkward fluency,
beautiful and ugly, the voice of a true-hearted
novice. The parrots also told Mike that his musical
enthusiasms left his father worried, which made
him practice more. Then there was an episode
where Mrs. Giggs said aloud to herself that Chico
knew what she had done, and gave Mike lessons
on the clarinet to punish her. The parrots revealed
this to the Judge, who had his own paroxysm, and
threw all kinds of furniture out the windows.

    The parrots repeated Mrs. Giggs' doubts
about Katherine, who she thought to be willful, a
sentimental fool. In response, the Judge had said
that it was her who instilled in young Katherine a
love of foreign things. His words were broadcast
through the house, by the parrots. Mrs. Giggs had
countered with her own accusations concerning
Charlie's death. The Judge replied that his wife
had insisted on this house, which preserved their
suffering. Meanwhile, Mike had groused about
the burden of replacing the dead favorite son, and
repeated his desire to kill the Swede boy. Katherine never said a word of what she thought, though
at night, in her sleep, she mingled Morgan's name
with moans of pain, and the parrots moaned with
her.

    Weeping seemed to issue from the walls, like
cries that cried themselves. Teach these fucking

birds to say Polly want a cracker, said the Judge to the Swede, before they drive us all insane. But the Bird Man had no power over birdspeech, and the parrots kept on talking.

After the monks had left with Mrs. Giggs, the Swede asked the Judge for a moment. Zvominir had figured that a confident and strong presentation would be best, for people valued strength, and he was usually too meek, perhaps to a fault. The Judge, full of smiles and goodwill that did not appear entirely sincere, clapped the Bird Man on the shoulder. What's on your mind, old friend, he asked.

Zvominir listed his troubles with Morgan, or rather, Morgan's troubles with the city, its duplicitous, exploitative, extortionist RedBlacks. We have been dependable, said Zvominir. Even when Morgan was beaten, he still went back to work. He simply needs protection, and equal opportunities. What with his loyal contribution to the city, it was time for the city to reciprocate.

Let him go to school in the suburbs, said Zvominir. Please. He needs to be safe, to have a normal life. I beg you.

The Judge revoked his phony smile, and said, No.

48

Mike, Tom and Gus sunned themselves on the lawn, along with the band and the families of the band, who now spent their days in the yard, with Mike's permission. They had all seen RedBlack doctors, and their medicine would be paid for by the city, on orders from Mike.

The tutor walked up to Mike, Tom and Gus. Follow me, he said. Leave the band. Take your guns.

They rode through flower-fields into the city, to the neighborhood where Katherine had her kitchen place, whatever the hell you called it, Mike had never seen it and didn't want to. For the longest time, he'd considered the city a giant prison, filled with only hopeless people, but now he liked the way the music seemed to float from store-fronts and bars, how solitary minstrels played on corners. He would have to spend more time down here, hearing music, maybe joining in.

Under the tutor's direction, Mike and Tom and Gus came to a bar. He told them to look as tough as possible, and to brandish their guns in such a way that it looked like they would use them. This might be worthwhile after all, Tom said. Fuckalallashitcock, said Gus, his favorite new word. Inside, the bar seemed dark—overdark—and stank of old beer. Mike thought all good times had this smell. A couple of guys shot pool, and the bartender stood by the register, counting his money. They entered the dirtiest bathroom Mike had ever seen. The tutor opened a stall and nudged a toilet with his boot, and, amazingly, the toilet swiveled on what must have been a hinge.

The next thing he saw was even stranger. Under the toilet was a ladder that descended into a sewer. The tutor led them down.

The tunnel was filled with Gypsies and their animals, Gypsies with instruments, Gypsies in a hurry, yelling or carrying bats, or weeping against the walls, among their children. Switch your safeties off, said the tutor.

Mike felt seasick. The Gypsies he knew from the barbecue were nothing like the rebel-looking men of the tunnels. He could be attacked at any moment, though bat-wielding Gypsies didn't notice him, thank god, so busy were they trilling and perspiring, or nodding to the music. The tunnel bent through concrete to an underground market, where more musicians played more songs, and men in feathered bird-suits danced as though attacked by bees. Mike had never felt so overwhelmed. Hundreds, maybe thousands of people heaved around him. He clutched his rifle to his body. Tom and Gus joked, looking happy in this madness. Mike wanted to go home. What are we doing, he asked.

There's something here you need to see.

They crawled into a tunnel filled with luminous old Gypsies, stored there like tools in a shed. Obsolete people were easy to push, but scary to look at. The tutor tapped the barrel of his rifle on
what looked like a sewer grate. Look in there, he said.

Mike pulled rags from the grate, and looked inside. He saw two people on what looked like a mattress. They were naked. They were Katherine
and Morgan.

49

When Mike couldn't yank the metal grate from the concrete, he and Tom and Gus shot their assault rifles at the concrete-and-earth around the black iron grid. Chunks of stone, smoke and ricocheting bullets sprayed like a geyser, and the tutor dove for cover behind the old Norwegians. Many of them toppled—collateral damage—blood splattering the walls. Shot-up nightplants bled a silver-colored, mercuryish goo. He plugged his ears against the noise, and gagged on smoke.

Inside the apartment, Morgan rolled on top of Katherine, to protect her, and they squirmed toward the door, where their clothes lay. Get the hell out of here, she said. It's probably Mike. He grabbed his pants, but left his shirt behind.

Mike kicked the smoldering stone around the grate, but it still wouldn't give, so he kept on shooting. Most of the Norwegians had died or staggered off, and the tutor lay concealed beneath a body-heap, thumbs in his ears. He watched as ricocheting bullets riddled Gus, watched him fall backwards and twitch, commence his death-throes; his soul was painfully extracted, and wrenched from every sinew.

The stone around the grate was blasted away, finally, and the grate clattered into the apartment.

Mike and Tom leaped in behind it, and the tutor climbed out from the bodies. He heard Katherine scream at Mike. The tutor leaped down into the apartment, saw that bullets had destroyed it, and the band leaped in behind him, brushing him aside. What the hell are you doing here, he asked. Mike said to tag along behind you guys, said Chico. Didn't you see us?

He shrugged, and scrambled off to find Mike. Katherine stood beside the door, covering her body with the clothes in her hands, looking tiny, dirty, small, defiant, weak, furious, delicate, beautiful and courageous. Courage, thought the tutor, is an actual thing.

I can't believe this, she said. You said you were different.

50 Morgan had a block-long head start on Mike and Tom, and he ran toward the slummiest, most dangerous city neighborhood, hoping they'd give up their chase, but they didn't, they shot at him and missed, and bystanders screamed; the flat cracks of gunshots and ricochets swirlingly echoed around him. Mike and Tom jumped onto anything that offered them an elevated view of the street—pushcarts, lampposts, stoops, awnings, horse-drawn carriages—nonetheless, they missed, killing nuns, little boys, mothers, donkeys, chickens, homeless men, schoolteachers, fathers, etc.

The tutor tried catching up to Mike and Tom as they tried catching Morgan, but he wasn't good at running, and he lagged, and shot badly, too, and missed worse than Mike, which is to say his victims were farther from Morgan than Mike and Tom's victims, his murders more random. The band played their music and caught up to Mike, and dodged alongside him through open-air markets, down alleys, through kitchens, restaurants, avenues, boulevards, squares and *piazzas*, playing their *ska*. Morgan had no shoes, he'd had no time to put them on. Mike refused to quit, and, judging from the sound of his band, he gained speed as he went. Morgan, who had prided himself in know-

ing the slums, was lost. He found himself running
down a boulevard of cypresses and whorehouses,
past heaps of stones and a lumberyard, and back
into a residential neighborhood, his way blocked
by donkey-drawn fruit-carts, the donkeys drop-
ping dead, shot by Mike.

He couldn't breath for gasping, stepped in
shit, and fell often on the cobblestones. He wondered why the gunshots had stopped. He didn't
see that Mike and Tom had used up their bullets,
that they'd flung away their guns and kept running. He ran for so long, but when he turned to
see if they had quit, they hadn't quit, they drew
closer, the pounding of the music gaining always
and steadily, implacable.

As he dodged between donkeys, he saw the
city's edge: the banks of the river now consumed
by venus flytraps. Has it really come to this? He
thought, Oh swans, the time is now to make my
offering. Please save my life. He leaped into the
waterless river, and found the ground of hard dirt.
He untied the knife from his ankle.

51

The zillion venus flytraps blinked their eagerness for spectacle as Mike and Tom confronted gasping Morgan. He raised his knife. He figured he would die. He wanted to embarrass death for taking him.

They were all out of breath. Mike and Tom had kicked his ass before, many times, but Mike felt different now, almost scared. Tom saw him hesitate, shrugged, said *banzai!* and flung himself at Morgan. The band started playing *Phoenix City*. Morgan swung his knife, slashing Tom's forearm, drawing blood, but Tom swerved and caught him in a chokehold. Tom had the knifehand now, and twisted it away; Morgan dropped the weapon. He kicked it away, to keep it from Tom, who could easily have gotten to it otherwise, but then he regretted getting rid of it, though what should he have done? Tom was stronger, Morgan barely held him off.

Tom punched Morgan in the face once, twice, three times, four times; Morgan lost count. He bled from below his left eye, the pain so great he almost fainted, and he staggered to the ground, and tried to crawl away through flytrap stalks, though Tom grabbed his foot and dragged him back to the clearing, and kicked him in the ribs with his boots. He could not defend himself. Tom knelt on top of him and choked him.

Darkness rose in Morgan's eyes, the flood of death. Desperately, he clawed at Tom's forearm, dug his nails into the wound, and pulled the flesh and veins off the bone. Tom screamed and staggered backward, his forearm gushing like a split pipe, opened like a sleeve unbuttoned.

You fucking piece of shit, Tom said, growling like a beast, you fucking piece of fucking shit, you motherless fucker, you mud-person. He set upon the smaller boy again, and hammered him with punches, and sprayed the plants with blood; they gulped it down. His strength had ebbed, though—his life poured out—and Morgan could defend against the softness of these blows, which only had the power of a branch.

Blood had stained the air and driven red into the clouds, the rags that marched along like parades, and the world would not recover. The band kept playing, and the singer, Johnny Steve, fell on his knees, leaped in the air, bobbed and weaved and sang, though he'd forgotten all the words. Morgan had time to rummage the weeds for the knife while Tom was busy dying. He picked it up and looked at Tom, a once-mighty boy who could hardly keep on his feet. He stabbed Tom in the heart, forced the blade between his ribs, fought through gristle, looked him in the eye. Murder was intimate. Tom spat blood, fell and died.

Morgan, drenched in gore, in a bodysuit of

blood, faced Mike, who appeared to be inching backwards. He pointed with the knife, but couldn't form a word. He appeared to be slobbering.

I don't want to die, Mike said. He turned and ran away.

The Worst Is Not So Long As We Can Say
"This Is The Worst"

52 The band followed Mike back to the city, their instruments all silent, except for a groaning tuba. They hoisted themselves to the shoreline, that riverwalk gone grimy, for who would want to look at venus flytraps, where once had flowed a river?

The streets had been abandoned in fear. Worried-looking birdclouds flew back and forth so nervously it seemed they'd pace a trough in the sky. The tutor arrived to the riverbank, finally, a posse of RedBlacks with him, who he'd gathered after giving up the chase. What the hell happened, he said to the band, or the three of them that hadn't wandered off. Morgan killed Tom, or was it Gus, I never did know the difference, said Clarence, the washboard player, and Mike ran away. Mike ran, said the tutor, I don't understand, what do you mean he ran? Ran from what? Ran from Morgan? The RedBlacks also looked surprised.

I guess he was afraid, said Clarence. Who knew he'd turn out to be a coward?

The tutor shot Clarence in the heart, and killed the other two musicians who were standing there: Zeke, who played the tenor sax, and Claude the bassist. Find the rest and kill them, said the tutor to the soldiers. They were part of the plot to assassinate Mike.

The RedBlacks looked confused. Part of
what?

Do it. said the tutor. Kill them all.

53 RedBlacks hunted the band block-to-block, storming into buildings, kicking doors in, shooting and interrogating, getting blank looks from Norwegians, or sneers that *Mike is a coward*. News of his disgrace had spread quickly; Norwegians insisted that Mike, not Morgan, had aggressed, that Morgan fought with courage and killed Mike's friends. RedBlacks smashed through the city, enraged at this failure of spin, insisting that the band had ambushed Mike, though nobody believed them, and, since RedBlacks had no flair for explanation or patience for debate, they shot those who dared contradict them. The Gypsies caught the drift and stopped talking, spoke but shrugs and muteness to the RedBlacks, a conspiracy of silence which helped conceal the band.

The RedBlacks resorted to pain.

The tutor told the Judge his version of the story, that the band had lured Mike into the tunnels, where Morgan launched an ambush. He sat before the Judge, who stood behind his desk, too furious to sit. The shimmering walls seemed worried, too. Mike fought with distinction, said the tutor, you have raised him to be brave. I don't need your encouragement, said the Judge, I'll reach my own conclusions without your help, and you were supposed to be protecting Mike, you're lucky I don't punish you for letting him into the tunnels, how dumb can you be? Mike's supposed to be the dumb one. I'm so sorry, said the tutor, My humblest apologies, and it's a good thing Mike used the techniques I taught him, which saved his life. Why, asked the Judge, do I read in reports that Mike ran away from Morgan. That sounds more like you, did he learn it from you? It's Norwegian propaganda, said the tutor. Your son was a hero.

They didn't speak of Katherine and Morgan. Nobody would dare write about them in a report. RedBlacks were furious at Mike for being scared, and were happy to embarrass him, but the sexual component of Katherine's transgression was too risqué to put to paper.

The Judge demanded to see his son. The tutor had coached the boy for this moment with his father, instructing Mike to say the band, in concert with Morgan, had lured and attacked him. I don't want to blame the band, Mike had said. Do you want to tell the truth, asked the tutor. You want to say you ran, that Morgan killed your friend and you did nothing? What about Katherine, Mike asked. It would probably be best to shut up about that.

The Judge told Mike to explain what had happened, and Mike obeyed the tutor. Morgan and the band attacked us, he said. He loved his band more than anything, and wanted to be with them now, running away from here. Officers hovered in the gloom, hardly visible, like figures in a drawing who'd been shaded by a pencil. They stood around the desk, already planning how to hunt and kill the band. Ancient-looking men who'd owned his name before him scowled down from their portraits. Then there was the portrait of the whole Giggs family, with Charlie smiling next to Katherine. It was also a lie. Nothing is real here, he thought, least of all me.

In the windows, trees appeared to mutter to each other. He had chased the band beneath these trees. We have to find the band and kill them, said the Judge. Have the tutor take you on the hunt. Don't be upset, he said, I'm very proud of you, son, for the first time in your life, you did good.

The singer and the banjoist were discovered in a closet, and murdered where they hid. The cellist was dragged from a dumpster and shot in an alley, and his brother, the accordion player, was killed in a bar. The promoter, who'd first approached Mike in the Square and whose name was Emir K, had somehow escaped. Families of the band were thrown in jail and never seen again. The drummers were caught at the border, trying to escape in a mule-cart, hidden in sacks of grain. The mule-carts were impounded, their owners were tortured, their grainsacks burned to ash with the bodies in them. The trumpeter, trombonist and alto saxophonist hid in the apart-

ment they shared, and wouldn't come out; Red-
Blacks destroyed the whole block. Other tenants
watched from the street as their homes and possessions were obliterated, and Mike looked with
them. Chico was discovered feeding starlings in a
park, and handcuffed to a tree until Mike and the
tutor arrived.

At the barbecue, Chico had insisted that Gypsies were honorable, which had pissed off the tutor ever since. Now, Chico had the gall not to run.
It was downright insinuating. Kill him, said the
tutor to the RedBlacks. Mike, get over here and
watch.

Why, Mike asked, in tears.

It'll prove you're not afraid.

Soldiers dragged the weeping Giggs boy to the
bench where Chico sat. Chico looked at Mike with
his smoky brown eyes. Mike had given Chico's
grandchildren piggy-back rides, had played the
clarinet with him, shared more joy with him than
any other person. Please, Chico begged. Please
don't do it. Fire, said the tutor.

Acknowledgements

The author has snickered at lengthy acknowledgements pages before, but finds he can't leave anyone off of his own, for many people helped him.

Thanks to Rikki Ducornet, Margaret Whitt, Jan Gorak, Janet Desaulniers, Carol Anshaw, James McManus, Paul Ashley, Robert Boswell, Toni Nelson, Kevin McIlvoy, Daniel Borzutzky, Ted Morgan, (for his name and other things) Andrew Zawacki, Judd Bloch, John Beer, Joel Craig, Greg Purcell, Susan Golomb, Corey Ferguson, Eve Herzog, Alex Ferguson, Aaron Burch, Elizabeth Ellen, David Brewer for the meatballs, Karen and Bruce and Charlie Gershman, Barbara Henderson, Jonathan Novy, Laura, Sam and Violet Novy, my parents, Fred and Susan Novy.

Last and most: Maura Brewer.